BOY IN THE TWILIGHT

Yu Hua

Boy in the Twilight

STORIES
OF THE
HIDDEN CHINA

TRANSLATED
FROM THE CHINESE
BY ALLAN H. BARR

PANTHEON BOOKS, NEW YORK

Translation copyright © 2014 by Allan H. Barr

All rights reserved. Published in the United States by Pantheon Books, a division of Random House LLC, New York, and in Canada by Random House of Canada Limited, Toronto, Penguin Random House Companies. Originally published in China as Huanghun li de nanhai, by Xin Shijie Chubanshe (New World Press), Beijing, in 1999.

Pantheon Books and colophon are registered trademarks of Random House LLC.

Selected stories in this work first appeared in the following: "Their Son" in Another Kind of Paradise, edited by Trevor Carolan (Boston: Cheng & Tsui, 2009); "Friends" in Asia Literary Review (Summer 2008); "No Name of My Own" in Dimsum: Asia's Literary Journal 10 (Spring 2005); "Victory" in The New Yorker (August 2013); "The Skipping-and-Stepping Game" in Persimmon: Asian Literature, Arts and Culture 4.2 (Summer 2003); "Appendix" and "Timid as a Mouse" in Words Without Borders (May 2004); "Timid as a Mouse" originally appeared in Chinese in Wo danxiao ru shu (Beijing: Xin Shijie Chubanshe, 1999).

Library of Congress Cataloging-in-Publication Data
Hua, Yu, [date]
[Huanghun li de nanhai. English]
Boy in the twilight : stories of the hidden China / Yu Hua ; Translated from the Chinese by Allan H. Barr.
p. cm.
Originally published in Chinese as Huanghun li de nanhai.
ISBN *978-0-307-37936-8*
I. Barr, Allan Hepburn, translator. II. Title.
PL2940.Y9H8313 2013 895.1'352—dc23 2013017450

www.pantheonbooks.com

Jacket image: Untitled, 2002, oil on paper, by Zhang Xiaogang. Courtesy of Pace Beijing. Jacket design by Linda Huang

Printed in the United States of America

First American Edition

1 3 5 7 9 10 8 6 4 2

CONTENTS

TRANSLATOR'S NOTE

Yu Hua published his first short story in 1983, when he was twenty-three. In the ebb and flow of his writing career since then, the early and mid-1990s stand out as an especially productive phase. Within the space of a few short years he completed a trio of novels—*Cries in the Drizzle, To Live,* and *Chronicle of a Blood Merchant*—that firmly established him as a major figure in the Chinese literary scene. The reputation of these books, particularly *To Live,* which was soon adapted for the screen by Zhang Yimou, has tended to overshadow the short fiction that Yu Hua published during this same period. But the stories collected here, all written between 1993 and 1998, represent a distinctive body of work in their own way. Written in a spare, minimalist style, they sketch vignettes of everyday life in contemporary China, in keeping with the "popular realism" that characterizes *To Live* and *Chronicle of a Blood Merchant.* If there is a recurrent theme in *Boy in the Twilight,* it is the fractures and fluidities in human relationships during the reform era in China: marriages in crisis collapse or rebound, friendships are cemented or betrayed, in a precarious world where events may take an unexpected turn at any time. Yet Yu Hua does not entirely abandon the unorthodox stance of his earlier fiction, and comic absurdity rubs shoulders with tragedy as these stories unfold.

BOY IN THE TWILIGHT

No Name of My Own

One day, as I crossed the bridge with my carrying-pole on my shoulder, I heard someone say that Pug-nose Xu Asan had died, so I laid down my baskets and took the towel that I wore around my neck and rubbed the sweat off my face while I listened to them talk about how it had happened, how Pug-nose Xu Asan choked to death eating New Year cake. I'd heard of someone choking to death on a peanut, but choking to death on New Year cake was a first as far as I knew. It was then they called me. "Xu Asan . . . Hey, Pug-nose . . ."

When I looked at the ground and went "Mm," they burst out laughing.

"What have you got in your hand?" they asked.

I looked at my hand. "Towel," I said.

There were gales of laughter. "What are you doing to your face?" someone asked.

"Rubbing the sweat off," I said.

I don't know why they were so happy. They were laughing so hard they swayed back and forth like reeds in the wind. "Wow, he can even say 'sweat'!" one of them spluttered, hand on his belly.

Another man was leaning back against the railing. "Xu Asan! Pug-nose Asan!" he cried.

Twice he said that, so I went "Mm" twice, too. "Who is Xu Asan?" he asked, clutching his gut.

I looked at him, and then at the other people next to him. Their mouths were gaping—their eyes too. "Yeah, who is Pug-nose Xu Asan?" they asked.

"Xu Asan is dead," I said.

Their goggling eyes blinked shut, but their mouths opened even wider. How loudly they laughed—louder still than the clang of iron in the smithy. A couple of them sat down on the ground, and after laughing helplessly for a while one asked me with a gasp, "Xu Asan is dead. So who are you?"

Who am I? I watched as they laughed fit to bust, unsure how to answer. I've got no name of my own, but as soon as I walk in the street I've got more names than anybody else. Whatever they want to call me, that's who I am. If they're sneezing when they run into me, they call me Sneeze; if they're coming out of the toilet, they call me Bum-wipe; when they want my attention, they call me Over-here; when they wave me away, they call me Clear-off . . . then there's Old Dog, Skinny Pig, and whatnot. Whatever they call me I answer to, because I've got no name of my own. All they need to do is take a few steps in my direction, look at me and call out a greeting, and I answer right away.

I thought of what to say. What people call me most often is Hey! So, hoping this was a good answer, I said, "I am . . . Hey!"

Their eyes widened. "*Who* are you?" they asked.

Perhaps I'd said the wrong thing. I looked at them, not daring to say more.

"Eh, what's that?" one asked again. "Who did you say you were?"

I shook my head. "I am . . . Hey."

They looked at each other and laughed, ha ha ha. I stood there and watched them laughing, and I began to laugh myself. People who were crossing the bridge saw us all laughing so loudly, and they joined in. Someone wearing a bright-colored shirt called out to me, "Hey!"

"Mm," I went.

The man in the bright shirt pointed at someone else. "Did you go to bed with his wife?" he asked.

I nodded. "Mm."

The other man started cursing. "You son of a bitch!"

Then he pointed at the man in the bright shirt. "You had a good time in bed with *his* wife, didn't you?" he said.

I nodded. "Mm."

Everybody had a big laugh. They often asked me this kind of thing, or asked if I'd slept with somebody's mother. Many years ago, when Mr. Chen was still alive—before Mr. Chen died, like Pug-nose Xu Asan—Mr. Chen, standing under the eaves, pointed his finger at me. "The way you people carry on," he said, "don't you realize you just end up making him look good? If you're to be believed, it would take several truckloads to carry all the women he's gone to bed with."

As I watched them laughing, I remembered what Mr. Chen said. "I went to bed with both your wives," I told them.

When they heard this, their smiles vanished right away and they stared at me. In a moment the man in the bright shirt came over, raised his fist, and hit me so hard my ears were buzzing for minutes afterward.

When Mr. Chen was still alive, he would often sit behind the counter of the pharmacy. There was a huge array of open or unopened little drawers behind his head and he would hold a little set of scales in those long, thin hands of his. Sometimes Mr. Chen would walk to the door of the pharmacy, and seeing me answer to any name I was called, he would say something.

He would say, "It's such a sin, what you people are doing, and still you get a kick out of it. There'll be a price to pay sooner or later. Everybody has a name, and he's got one too, his name is Laifa."

When Mr. Chen mentioned my name, when he said I was Laifa, my heart would skip a beat. I remember when my dad was alive, how he'd sit on the threshold and tell me things. "Laifa," he'd say, "bring the teapot over here."

"Laifa, now you're five . . ."

"Laifa, here's a satchel for you."

"Laifa, you're ten already, but still in first grade, damn it."

"Laifa, forget about school, help your dad carry coal."

"Laifa, just another few years and you'll be as strong as I am."

"Laifa, your dad's not got long to live, not long now—the doctor says I've got a tumor in my lung."

"Laifa, don't cry. Laifa, when I'm gone you won't have your mom, or your dad either."

"Laifa, Lai . . . fa, Lai . . . , Lai . . . fa, . . . Laifa, your dad is dying . . . Laifa, feel here, your dad is getting stiff . . . Laifa, look, your dad's looking at you . . ."

After my dad died, I made my rounds and walked the streets, delivering coal to people all around town. "Laifa, where's your dad?" they would ask.

"He died," I said.

They would chuckle. "Laifa, what about your mom?"

"She died," I said.

"Laifa, are you a halfwit?"

I nodded. "I'm a halfwit."

When my dad was alive, he would say to me, "Laifa, you're

a simpleton. You were in school for three years, but you still can't recognize a single character. Laifa, it's not your fault, it's your mom's fault. When she was giving birth, she squeezed your head too tight. Laifa, it's not your mom's fault either. Your head was too big, you were the death of her . . ."

"LAIFA, HOW DID YOUR MOM DIE?" they asked.
   "She died in childbirth," I said.
   "Which child was that?" they asked.
   "Me," I said.
   "How did she give birth to you?" they asked again.
   "With one foot in the coffin," I said.
   Hearing this, they would laugh a good long time. "What about the other foot?"
   I wasn't sure about the other foot. Mr. Chen didn't tell me—all he said was, when a woman gives birth she has one foot in the coffin. He didn't say where she puts the other one.

"HEY, WHO'S YOUR DADDY?" they shouted.
   "My daddy died," I said.
   "Nonsense," they said, "your daddy's alive and well."
   I looked at them, eyes wide. They came over, close to me, and whispered in my ear. "I'm your daddy."
   I looked down and thought for a moment. "Mm," I went.
   "Am I your daddy?" they asked.
   I nodded. "Mm."
   I heard them chortle. Mr. Chen came over. "Pay no attention to them," he said. "You've only got one dad. Everybody's only got one dad. If people had lots of different dads, how would their moms manage?"

. . .

AFTER MY DAD DIED, the people in the town, no matter how old they were—the men, I mean—practically all of them told me they were my dad. With so many dads, I started having lots of names, and I didn't have enough fingers in the evening to count all the new names they gave me during the day.

Only Mr. Chen still called me Laifa. Every time I saw Mr. Chen and heard him call my name, my heart would skip a beat. Mr. Chen would stand in the doorway of the pharmacy, watching me with his hands inside his sleeves, and I would stand there and look at him back. Sometimes it made me snicker. After a while Mr. Chen would wave me away, saying, "Off you go. Look, you've still got a load of coal on your back."

One time, I didn't go off. I just stood there. "Mr. Chen," I went.

Mr. Chen's hands came out of his sleeves and he stared at me. "What did you call me?"

My heart was thumping. Mr. Chen came over. "What did you say just now?"

"Mr. Chen," I said.

He smiled. "You're not so dumb, after all," he said. "You know to call me Mr. Chen, Laifa."

He called my name again and I smiled just as Mr. Chen had done. "Do you know that Laifa is your name?" he asked.

"Yes," I said.

"Let me hear you say it."

"Laifa," I said quietly.

That made Mr. Chen laugh very hard, and I opened my mouth and joined in. After a little more laughing, Mr. Chen said, "Laifa, from now on, unless people call you Laifa, just don't answer them, do you understand?"

I smiled. "I understand," I said.

Mr. Chen nodded. Then, looking at me, he called, "Mr. Chen."

"Mm," I went.

"When I call my own name, why do you answer?"

I didn't know Mr. Chen was calling his own name. I thought it was funny, so I smiled. He shook his head. "You're still a simpleton, it seems."

MR. CHEN DIED a long time ago, and Pug-nose Xu Asan died just a few days ago, and a lot of people died in between. People around the same age as Xu Asan have white hair and white beards, and these days I often hear them saying they'll soon be dead, so I think I'll be dead myself soon, too. They tell me I'm older than Pug-nose Xu Asan. "Hey, idiot," they say, "who's going to collect your body once you're dead?"

I shake my head. I really don't know who's going to bury me once I'm dead. I ask them who will bury them when they're dead, and they say, "We've got sons and grandsons, wives too. Our wives aren't dead yet. What about you? Have you got sons? Have you got grandsons? You don't even have a wife."

I said nothing. I haven't got any of those people, so I put my load on my back and went on my way. But Xu Asan had all those people. The day that Pug-nose Xu Asan was cremated, I saw his son and grandson and all the women weeping and wailing as they walked along the street. I followed them to the crematorium with my empty load on my back. It was a lively scene all the way, and I thought how nice it would be if I had a son and a grandson and other family. I walked along next to Xu Asan's grandson. The kid was crying louder than anyone, but he asked me as he wept, "Hey, am I your daddy?"

PEOPLE ABOUT THE SAME AGE as me are tired of being my dad now. They used to give me all kinds of names, but sooner or later they put the question to me point-blank, they ask me what my name is. They say, "What *is* your name? When you die, we want to know who it is has died . . . Think about it: when Xu Asan died, all we needed to do was to say Xu Asan died, and everyone would understand, but what do we say when you die? You've got no name at all."

I know what my name is. My name is Laifa. It used to be that Mr. Chen was the only person who remembered my name, and once he died, nobody knew my name. Now they all want to know what I'm called, but I won't tell them. They roar with laughter and they say: An idiot is just an idiot pure and simple. He's an idiot in life and an idiot when he's lying dead in his coffin.

I know I'm an idiot. I know I'm getting old and will die soon. Sometimes I think: It's true what they say. I don't have a son or a grandson, and when I die nobody will weep and wail and see me off to my cremation. I still don't have a name of my own, and once I'm dead they won't know who has died.

These days I often think of that dog I used to have, that skinny little dog that later grew up to be big and strong. They used to call it Dummy, too. I knew they were cursing it when they called it Dummy. I didn't call it that. I called it Hey.

In those days streets weren't as wide as they are now, and houses weren't as tall. Mr. Chen would stand in the doorway of the pharmacy. His hair was still black then. Even Pug-nose Xu

Asan was young in those days. It was before he was married. "A man like me, in his twenties . . . ," he would say.

But my dad was dead. I had been delivering coal on my own for years by then. As I walked along the street, I'd often see that dog, so small and skinny, mouth open, tongue hanging out, licking this and that, wet all over. I'd seen it around a lot, so when Pug-nose Xu Asan lifted it up and showed it to me that time, I recognized it right away. Xu Asan had stopped me in the street. He and a few other people were standing outside his house, and Xu Asan said, "Hey, do you want to get married?"

I stood on the other side of the street and watched them snickering, and I snickered myself. "The dummy wants a woman," they said. "He smiled."

"Do you want to get married or not?" Xu Asan asked.

"What for?" I said.

"What for? To live with you . . . sleep with you, have meals with you . . . Would you like that or not?"

I nodded. That's when they brought out the dog. Xu Asan picked it up by the scruff of its neck and thrust it toward me. Its four legs were scrabbling around and it was barking madly. "Hey, hurry up and take her. She's yours," he said.

They stood there, roaring with laughter. "Come on, dummy! Come and collect your mate."

I shook my head. "That's no woman."

Xu Asan shouted at me, "If it's not a woman, what is it?"

"It's a dog, it's a puppy," I said.

They roared with laughter. "This dummy knows about dogs . . . He knows about puppies."

"Rubbish." Xu Asan glared at me. "This is a female, look here . . ."

Xu Asan lifted the dog's rear legs and yanked them apart to show me. "Did you get a good look?" he asked.

I nodded. "Female, right?" he said.

I shook my head again. "It's not a woman," I said. "It's a bitch."

They went off into gales of laughter, and Pug-nose Xu Asan laughed so hard he had to squat down. The dog's rear legs were still clamped between his hands, and it barked furiously as its head scraped the ground. I just stood there with a smile on my face. After a moment Xu Asan stood up again and pointed at me. "He could tell this dog is a bitch," he said to the others. Then he squatted down and cackled as loud as a cicada chirping. As soon as he relaxed his grip, the dog dashed off.

From that day on, whenever Pug-nose Asan and the others saw me, they would say, "Hey, your girlfriend . . . Hey, your girlfriend fell into the cesspit . . . Hey, your girlfriend is having a piss . . . Hey, your girlfriend pinched some meat from my house . . . Hey, looks like your girlfriend's pregnant . . ."

They were laughing away nonstop. When I saw what a good time they were having, I laughed along with them. I knew they were talking about the dog. They were looking forward to the day when I would take that dog into my house as though she were a woman and spend my life with her.

Day after day they would talk that way, and every time they would look at me and go ha-ha and tee-hee. So the next time I saw the dog, I felt kind of funny. The dog was as small and skinny as ever, its tongue always hanging out, licking this and that in the street. I would walk past with my load on my back, and when I got close I couldn't help but stop and look. One day, quietly, I called it. I said, "Hey."

When it heard me, it gave a few barks, so I offered it half a steamed bun left over from lunch. It grabbed the bun between its teeth and ran off.

After I fed it that half bun, it remembered me, and every time it saw me it would bark and I'd have to give it a bun. Once this happened a few times, I remembered to stuff my pockets with things to eat, so I could make it happy when we met in the street. And as soon as it saw me put my hand in my pocket, it knew what was coming and would raise its front legs and bark and jump up on me.

Later, the dog would tag along with me every day. I would walk in front carrying my load, and it would patter along behind. At the end of the block I would look back and there it would be, barking and wagging its tail. A block later, there would be no sign of it and I wouldn't know where it had gone. I'd wait for a while, and suddenly it would appear and start following me once more. Sometimes it would run away and not come back until after dark. I would already be in bed, and it would run back, sit outside my door and bark. I'd have to open the door and show myself, and then it would stop barking, wag its tail, and patter away again.

When I was walking along the street with the dog at my heels, Pug-nose Xu Asan and the others would chuckle. "Hey, out for a stroll with the wife, are you?" they'd say. "Hey, are the two of you going home now? Hey, when you're in bed together, who cuddles who?"

"We don't spend the night together," I'd tell them.

"Nonsense," Xu Asan would say. "Husband and wife are always together at night."

"We're not," I said.

"You dummy," they said. "That's the whole point of being a couple."

Xu Asan made as though to turn off a light. "Click! When the light goes off, that's when the fun starts."

Pug-nose Xu Asan and the others wanted me and the dog to be together at night, and I thought about that, but it never worked out that way. As soon as it got dark, the dog would patter off and I didn't know where it went. It would come back at dawn, scratch on the door, and wait for me to open it.

But during the day we'd be together, me carrying the coal and it walking by my side. When I made a delivery, it would roam around the neighborhood, and when I came out it would soon catch up with me.

After a few days, the dog got rounder and plumper, and grew taller too. When it ran alongside, I could see its belly swing back and forth. Xu Asan and the others noticed this too. "This bitch, have a look at this plump little bitch," they'd say.

One day they stopped me in the street and Xu Asan pulled a long face. "Hey, how come we haven't got our candy yet?" he said.

The dog barked when they blocked my path. They pointed at the shop across the street. "Do you see that?" they said. "The glass jar on the counter, the one with all the candy in it? See it? Off you go."

"What for?" I said.

"To buy candy," they said.

"Why candy?" I said.

"For us to eat," they said.

"Damn it," Xu Asan said, "you haven't given us the wedding candy yet! Wedding candy! Don't you get it? We were your matchmakers, weren't we?"

So saying, they stuck their hands in my pockets and groped around for some change. This got the dog all riled up; it was growling and lunging. When Xu Asan aimed a kick at it, it ran a few paces back, barking away, and when he took two steps closer, it dashed off. They found some cash in my chest pocket, helped themselves to two twenty-fen notes, and stuffed the rest back. Holding my money aloft, they crowded into the shop opposite. The dog ran back as soon as they were gone, and scampered away again as soon as they came out. Xu Asan and the others stuffed a few bits of candy in my hand. "This is for the happy couple," they said.

Off they went, laughing and chewing their candy. By this time it was almost dark, and I headed home clutching the candy they'd given me. The dog raced back and forth, now ahead, now behind, barking madly and making a lot of noise. It barked all the way home, and didn't stop even when we reached the door. It stood there and didn't seem to want to leave, its head cocked, looking up at me. "Hey, stop that barking," I said, but it just kept on. "Why don't you come in?" I said.

It didn't move and just carried on yowling. But when I waved my hand, it stopped all its ruckus and trotted inside.

From then on, the dog lived in my house. I went and got a pile of straw and laid it in the corner of the room: that was its bed. I thought it over that evening and felt that having a dog move into your house really was a bit like taking a wife. In the future I would have a companion, just as Mr. Chen said. "Finding a companion, that's what marriage is," he used to say.

"They say we're man and wife," I said, "but a man and a dog can't be husband and wife. The most we can be is companions."

I sat down on the straw, next to my dog. It gave a couple

of barks. I smiled and laughed, and on hearing me it barked a little more. I smiled and laughed again, and it barked again. So we went on like that for a while, me laughing, it barking, until I remembered I still had candy in my pocket, so I got it out and peeled off the wrapper. "This is candy, wedding candy, that's what they said . . ."

When I heard myself say it was wedding candy, I couldn't help but smile. I peeled off a couple of wrappers, and put one candy in the dog's mouth and one in mine. "How does it taste?" I said.

I could hear it chewing noisily, and I chewed my candy too, even more noisily. We chewed away and it made me laugh. As soon as I did that, it started barking again.

In our two years together, the dog went with me everywhere. When I lifted my load onto my shoulders it would run ahead barking, and when my baskets were empty it would trot along a step or two behind. Seeing us, people in the town would chuckle. They would point and say, "Hey, are you husband and wife?"

I went "Mm," walking on ahead with my head down.

"Hey, are you a dog?"

When I went "Mm," they would start shouting. "Hey, dummy! Hey, dumb dog! Hey, dogface! Hey, dog-fuck! Or is it dog-fucker? Hey, when are you going to be a dog-dad?"

I just went "Mm" to everything. "You're a man, aren't you?" Mr. Chen asked. "What's all this about you and the dog being husband and wife?"

I shook my head. "Man and dog can't be husband and wife," I said.

"As long as you're clear about that," said Mr. Chen. "In the future, if anybody calls you that kind of name, don't do that 'Mm, mm' stuff."

I nodded. "Mm," I went.

"Don't keep going 'Mm,' just remember what I told you," he said.

I nodded and went "Mm" again. He waved me away. "Okay, okay, off you go," he said.

I walked off, carrying my load, and the dog pattered along in front of me. It seemed to be putting on a bit more weight every day. Before long it had grown up big and strong, and it began to get ideas. Sometimes I wouldn't see it for a whole day at a time, and I didn't know where it had gone off to. It wouldn't come back until after dark. It would scratch the door, I would open up, and it would slip in and lie down on the straw in the corner. It would put its head on the floor and look at me out of the corners of its eyes, and I would say, "The day before yesterday, when I got to the rice store, I turned around and you were gone, and yesterday when I got to the furniture shop I turned around and you were gone, and today when I got to the pharmacy I turned my head and you were gone . . ."

Before I finished speaking, the dog's eyes would be closed. I had a think, and closed my eyes too . . .

As my dog grew taller, it got nice and plump, and when Pug-nose Xu Asan and the others saw me they would say, "Hey, halfwit, when are we going to slaughter the dog?"

They were drooling at the mouth. "When it snows," they said, "we'll slaughter it, add water and soy sauce, cinnamon and the five spices . . . Braise it slowly for a whole day. It'll taste so damn good."

When I knew they wanted to eat my dog, I quickly picked up my load and went on my way, the dog running along by my side. I remembered what they'd said, how they'd eat my dog when it snowed. "When is it going to snow?" I asked Mr. Chen.

"That's a long time from now," Mr. Chen said. "You're still wearing a T-shirt. You need to wait till you're wearing a padded jacket."

When Mr. Chen said that, I didn't feel so anxious. But what happened was, before I had started wearing a padded jacket, before the snow came, Pug-nose Xu Asan and the others already wanted to eat my dog. They got a bone and tricked it into Xu Asan's house, and then they shut the door and closed the windows and started beating my dog with sticks, trying to kill my dog, so they could braise it on the stove for a day.

My dog knew they wanted to kill and eat it, so it hid underneath Xu Asan's bed and wouldn't come out. Xu Asan and the others poked it with their sticks, and it barked so loud I heard it when I was doing my rounds.

That morning I looked over my shoulder when I reached the bridge, and the dog was nowhere to be seen. In the afternoon I heard it barking furiously as I walked past Xu Asan's house, so I came to a stop and was standing by the door when Xu Asan and the others came out. "Hey, halfwit, we were just about to look for you," they said. "Hey, halfwit, hurry up and tell your dog to come out."

They thrust a looped rope into my hands. "Put this around the dog's neck and strangle it," they said.

I shook my head and pushed the lasso away. "It hasn't snowed yet," I said.

"What's the halfwit saying?" they asked each other.

"He says it hasn't snowed yet."

"What does he mean it hasn't snowed yet?"

"No idea," they said. "To know that, you'd have to be a half-wit too."

I could hear the dog barking inside, and there were people poking it with sticks. Xu Asan patted me on the shoulder. "Hey buddy, hurry up and tell the dog to come out."

They dragged me over there. "What are you calling him buddy for?" they said. "Cut the crap . . . Take this rope . . . and strangle the dog . . . You won't? You'd better, or we'll strangle *you* next."

Xu Asan blocked their way. "He's a halfwit. There's no point in trying to scare him, he won't understand. We need to trick him . . ."

"Tricking him won't work," they said. "He still won't understand."

I saw Mr. Chen walking over. He had his hands in his pockets and was walking slowly, step by step.

"Let's just take the bed apart," they said. "Then the dog will have no place to hide."

"We can't take the bed apart," Xu Asan said. "The dog's already in a panic. If it feels any more threatened, it'll bite."

"You dog, you mangy dog . . . ," they said to me. "Yeah, it's you we're talking to. Why don't you hurry up and answer?"

I bent my head and went "Mm" a couple of times. Mr. Chen spoke up off to one side. "If you want him to help," he said, "you need to call him by his real name. If you keep on using bad words and cursing him, he's never going to help. You say he's a halfwit, but he's not always such a fool."

"You're right," said Xu Asan, "let's call him by his real name.

Who knows his real name? What's he called? What's this half-wit's name?"

"Do you know, Mr. Chen?" they asked.

"Of course I know," he said.

Xu Asan and the others surrounded him. "Mr. Chen, what's this halfwit's name?" they asked.

"His name is Laifa."

When I heard that, my heart skipped a beat. Xu Asan came up to me and put his arm on my shoulder. "Laifa," he said.

My heart began to thump. Xu Asan, his arm around me, walked me toward his house. "Laifa, we're old pals . . . Laifa, go and tell your dog to come out . . . Laifa, all you need to do is walk over to the bed . . . Laifa, just call it nicely now . . . Laifa, just say 'Hey' . . . Laifa, I'm counting on you."

I went into Xu Asan's bedroom, squatted down, and saw my dog lying prone beneath the bed. There was blood all over it. I called it gently. "Hey."

As soon as it heard my voice, it scurried out and threw its paws on me, butting me with its head and chest, so my face was smeared with blood. It gave a baying noise, a baying noise I'd never heard it make before, and that upset me a lot. I reached over to give it a hug, and no sooner did I hold it close to me than they put the rope around its neck. With a tug they dragged it out of my arms. Before I realized it, the hands that were hugging the dog were empty. I heard it give a little woof, just a little woof, that's all, and I saw its four feet scrabble on the ground for a little, and then it didn't move anymore. "It hasn't snowed yet!" I said, as they dragged it away.

They looked at me and laughed.

That evening I sat by myself on the straw where the dog

used to sleep. I thought about the whole thing. I knew my dog was dead. I knew they'd poured water over it, and soy sauce and cinnamon and the five spices, and now they'd braise it over a fire for a day and tomorrow they'd eat it.

I thought about this for a long time. I knew that it was my fault the dog died. It got strangled because I coaxed it out from under Xu Asan's bed. My heart thumped when they called me Laifa, and that was all it took to get me to do what they said. I shook my head when I remembered that, and shook it for a good long time. "Next time somebody calls me Laifa," I said to myself, "I'm just not going to answer them."

BOY IN THE TWILIGHT

It was the middle of an autumn day. Sun Fu sat beside a fruit stand, his eyes squinting in the bright sunshine. He leaned forward, hands on his knees, and his grizzled hair seemed gray in the sunlight, gray like the road that lay before him, a wide road that extended from the far distance and then stretched off in the other direction. He had occupied this spot for three years now, selling fruit near where the long-haul buses stopped. When a car drove by, it shrouded him in the dust stirred by its passage, plunging him into darkness, and it was a moment before he and his fruit re-emerged, as though unveiled by a new dawn.

After the cloud of dust had passed, he saw an urchin in dirty clothes in front of the stall, watching him with dark, gleaming eyes. As he returned the boy's gaze, the boy put a hand on the fruit, a hand with long black fingernails. When he saw the nails brush against a shiny red apple, Sun Fu raised his hand to wave him away, the way he would swat away a fly. "Clear off," he said.

The boy withdrew his grubby hand and swayed a little as he shuffled off, his arms hanging slack at his sides. On such a skinny body his head looked oversized.

Others were now approaching the stand, and Sun Fu turned to look. They stopped on the other side of the stall and threw him a glance. "How much are the apples?" they asked. "How much for a pound of bananas?"

Sun Fu stood up, weighed apples and bananas on his steelyard, and took their money. Then he sat down and put his hands on his knees. The boy had come back. This time he was not standing directly in front, but off to one side, his glowing eyes fixed on the apples and bananas, as Sun Fu watched him with equal attention. After gazing at the fruit for a while, the boy looked up at Sun Fu. "I'm hungry," he said.

Sun Fu was silent. "I'm hungry," the boy repeated, a note of urgency creeping into his voice.

Sun Fu scowled. "Clear off."

The boy's body seemed to give a shiver. "Clear off," Sun Fu said again, more loudly.

The boy gave a start. His body swayed hesitantly before his legs began to move. Sun Fu took his eyes off the boy and switched his attention to the highway. A long-haul bus had come to a halt on the other side of the road, and the people inside stood up. Through the bus windows, he could see a column of shoulders crowding toward the doors; a moment later, passengers poured from both ends of the bus. Then, out of the corner of his eye, Sun Fu saw the boy dashing off as fast as his legs could carry him. He wondered why, and then he saw the boy's flailing hand: it was clutching something, something round. Now he recognized what it was. He leapt to his feet and set off in chase. "Stop thief!" he shouted. "Stop that thief there."

It was afternoon now. Dust flew as the boy fled along the highway. He heard shouting behind him, and looked round to see Sun Fu in hot pursuit. He floundered on desperately, gasping for breath, and when his legs began to go soft he knew he had no more reserves of energy. Looking back a second time, he saw Sun Fu still on his tail, yelling and waving his arms furiously. All hope gone, the boy came to a stop and turned around, panting heavily. He watched until Sun Fu was almost on top of him and then raised the apple to his mouth and took a big bite out of it.

Sun Fu swung his arm and struck the boy, knocking the apple out of his hand and connecting so firmly with the boy's chin that he collapsed on the ground. He shielded his head with his hands, all the time chewing vigorously. Sun Fu, incensed, seized the boy by the collar and hauled him to his feet. The boy's throat was so constricted by the tight collar that it was impossible for him to chew; his eyes began to goggle and his cheeks swelled, some apple still inside. Gripping the collar with one hand, Sun Fu squeezed the boy's neck with the other. "Spit it out! Spit it out!" he yelled.

A crowd was gathering. "He's still trying to eat it!" Sun Fu told them. "He stole my apple and took a bite out of it, and now he's trying to swallow it!"

Sun Fu slapped him hard on the face. "Come on, spit it out."

But the boy simply clenched his mouth all the more firmly. Sun Fu put a hand on his throat and started throttling him once more. "Spit it out!" he cried.

As the boy's mouth opened, Sun Fu could see chewed-up bits of apple inside. He tightened his viselike grip on the boy's throat, until his eyes began to bulge. "Sun Fu," somebody said, "look, his eyeballs are practically popping out of his head. You're going to strangle him."

"Serves him right," Sun Fu said. "It serves him right if he's strangled."

Finally, he loosened his hold. "If there's one thing I hate," he said, pointing at the sky, "it's a thief. Spit it out!"

The boy began to spit out the apple piece by piece. It was a bit like squeezing toothpaste out of a tube, the way he spat bits onto his shirt front. After he closed his mouth, Sun Fu levered it open again with his hand, and bent down to look inside. "You haven't spit it all out," he said. "There's still some left."

The boy spat again—practically all saliva this time, but with a few crumbs of apple here and there. The boy spat and spat, until in the end there was just a dry noise, no saliva anymore. "That'll do," Sun Fu said.

He saw many familiar faces among the people who had gathered to watch. "In the old days we never locked our doors, did we?" he said. "There wasn't a family in the whole town that locked its doors, was there?"

He saw people nodding. "Now, after locking the door once, you have to use a second lock as well," he continued. "Why? It's because of thieves like this. If there's one thing I hate, it's a thief."

Sun Fu looked at the grimy-faced boy, who watched spellbound, as though fascinated by what he was saying. The boy's expression stirred an excitement in him. "If we follow the old ways," he said, "we ought to break one of his hands, break the hand that did the stealing . . ."

Sun Fu looked down at the boy. "Which hand was it?" he shouted.

The boy shivered and hastily put his right hand behind his back. Sun Fu grabbed the hand and showed it to everybody. "It was this hand. Otherwise, why would he try to hide it so quickly?"

"It wasn't that hand!" the boy cried.

"Then it was this hand." Sun Fu grabbed the boy's left hand.

"No, it wasn't!"

As he said this, the boy tried to pull his hand away. Sun Fu gave him a slap on the face that made him teeter. After a second slap, the boy stood still. Sun Fu grabbed him by the hair, jerking his head up. "Which hand was it?" he yelled, staring into his face.

The boy's eyes widened as he looked at Sun Fu, and after a moment he stretched out his right hand. Sun Fu took hold of the boy's wrist, and with his other hand gripped the middle finger of the boy's hand. "If we follow the old ways," he said to the bystanders, "we should break this hand. We can't do that anymore. Now we emphasize education. How do we educate?"

Sun Fu looked at the boy. "This is how we educate."

He pressed down hard with both hands. There was a sudden crack as he broke the boy's middle finger. The boy screamed with a cry as sharp as a knife. Looking down, he saw the broken digit flopping against the back of his hand and slumped to the ground in shock.

"That's the way to deal with thieves," Sun Fu said. "If you don't break one of their arms, at the very least you need to break a finger."

Saying this, Sun Fu leaned down and hauled the boy to his feet. He noticed the boy's eyes were clamped shut with pain. "Open your eyes!" he yelled. "Come on, open them."

The boy opened his eyes, but he was still in agony and his mouth was twisted into a strange shape. Sun Fu kicked him in the legs. "Move it!"

Sun Fu grabbed him by the collar and shoved him along the street until they were back in front of the fruit stand. He rummaged around in a carton for some rope and tied him to the stall. "Shout," he said to the boy, when he saw people watching. "Shout 'I'm a thief!'"

The boy looked at Sun Fu. When he failed to comply, Sun Fu seized his left hand and took a tight grip on the left middle finger. "I'm a thief!" the boy cried.

"That's not loud enough," Sun Fu said. "Louder."

The boy looked at Sun Fu, then thrust his head forward and yelled with all his might, "I'm a thief!"

Sun Fu saw how the blood vessels on the boy's neck protruded. He nodded. "That's good," he said. "That's the way you need to shout."

All afternoon the autumn sun bathed the boy in light. His two hands were tied behind his back and the rope was coiled around his neck, so it was impossible for him to lower his head. He had no choice but to stand there stiffly, his eyes on the highway. Beside him lay the fruit that he had coveted, but with his neck fixed in place he could not even give it a glance. Whenever someone walked by—any passerby at all—at Sun Fu's insistence he would shout, "I'm a thief!"

Sun Fu sat behind the fruit stand on his stool, watching the boy contentedly. He was no longer so indignant about losing an apple and had begun to feel pleased with a job well done, because he had captured and punished the apple thief, and the punishment was still not over. He made sure the boy yelled at the top of his voice every time somebody walked by. He had noticed the boy's shouts were drawing a constant flow of people to his fruit stand.

Many looked with curiosity at the yelling boy. They found it strange that a trussed-up captive would cry "I'm a thief" so vigorously. Sun Fu filled them in on the story, tirelessly explaining how the boy had stolen an apple, how he'd been caught, and how he was being punished. "It's for his own good," Sun Fu would add.

And he'd make clear the thinking behind this. "I want him to understand he must never steal again."

Then Sun Fu would turn to the boy. "Are you going to do any more stealing?" he barked.

The boy shook his head vehemently. Because his neck was clamped so tight, he shook his head only slightly, but very quickly.

"Did you see that?" Sun Fu said triumphantly.

All afternoon long, the boy shouted and yelled. His lips dried and cracked in the sun and his voice grew hoarse. By dusk, the boy was unable to come out with a full-blown shout and could only make a scraping noise, but still he went on crying, "I'm a thief."

The passersby could no longer make out what it was he was shouting. "He's shouting 'I'm a thief,'" Sun Fu said.

After that, Sun Fu untied the rope. It was almost dark now. Sun Fu transferred the fruit to his flatbed cart, and when everything was in order he untied his prisoner. Just as Sun Fu was placing the coiled rope on top of the cart, he heard a dull thump behind him and looked round to find the boy had crumpled to the ground. "After this," he said, "I bet you won't dare to steal again, will you?"

As he spoke, Sun Fu mounted the bicycle at the front of the cart and rode off down the broad highway, leaving the boy sprawled on the ground. Weakened by hunger and thirst, he had collapsed as soon as he was untied. Now he just went on lying there, his eyes slightly ajar, as though looking at the road, or as though not looking at anything at all. He lay motionless for some minutes, and then he slowly clambered to his feet and propped himself against a tree. Finally, he started shuffling down the road, toward the west.

Westward the boy headed, his puny body swaying slightly in the twilight as he made his way out of town one step at a time. Some witnessed his departure and knew he was the thief Sun Fu had caught that afternoon, but they didn't know his name or where he had come from, and of course they had even less idea where he was going. They saw how his middle finger dangled against the back of his right hand, and watched as he trudged into the distant twilight and disappeared.

That evening, as usual, Sun Fu went to the little shop next door to buy a pint of rice wine, then cooked himself a couple of simple dishes and sat down at the square dining table. At this hour of the day the setting sun shone in through the window and seemed to warm the room up. Sun Fu sat there in the twilight, sipping his wine.

Many years ago, he had shared the room with a pretty woman and a five-year-old boy. In those days the room was constantly buzzing with noise and activity, and there was no end of things for the three of them to talk about. Sometimes he would simply sit inside and watch as his wife lit a fire outside in the coal stove. Their son would stick to her like toffee, tugging on her jacket and asking or telling her something in his shrill little voice.

Later, one summer lunchtime, some boys ran in, shouting Sun Fu's name. They said his son had fallen into a pond not far away. He ran like a man possessed, his wife following behind with piercing wails. Before long it was all too clear that they had lost their son forever. That night they sat together sobbing and moaning in the darkness and the stifling heat.

Later on still, they began to regain their composure, carrying on their lives as they had before, and in this way several years quickly passed. Then, one winter, an itinerant barber stopped outside their house. Sun Fu's wife went out, sat in the chair that the barber provided, closed her eyes in the bright sunshine, and let the barber wash and cut her hair, clean her ears, and massage her arms and shoulders. She had never in her life felt so relaxed as she did that day: it was as though her whole body was melting away. Afterward she stuffed her clothes into a bag and waited until the sky was dark, then set off along the route the barber had taken.

Sun Fu was alone now, his past condensed into the faded black-and-white photo that hung on the wall. It was a family portrait: himself, his wife, and their son. The boy was in the middle, wearing a cotton cap several sizes too big. On the left, in braids, his wife smiled blissfully. Sun Fu was on the right, his youthful face brimming with life.

looking at him. Then, after we had pretty much forgotten he was there, Lü Yuan suddenly gave a cry of astonishment. Her eyes bulging, she pointed a finger at Horsie's table setting. It was then we noticed a row of shrimp, five in all, big and small alike, lined up in front of him. Transparent shrimp shells lay sparkling in the light, deposited back on the plate by Horsie after he had cleanly extracted the meat inside. Seeing this, the other two girls gasped with surprise.

Horsie then picked up the last shrimp on the platter. His arm stretched across the table at the same height as his lowered head, and when his chopsticks gripped the shrimp, his elbow twitched with the speed of a lobster's pincers and he deposited the shrimp in his mouth.

Now he raised his head, and calmly looked at us flabbergasted spectators. His lips closed, his cheeks bulged, his mouth wriggled like an intestine, and his Adam's apple made a fluid up-and-down movement. Eventually, his bulging cheeks contracted and his Adam's apple rose. It lingered a moment in that elevated position as he swallowed, a cautious, dignified expression on his face.

His Adam's apple slipped down and his mouth opened. Then came the moment that left us stupefied: he disgorged what appeared to be a complete and undamaged shrimp, but—and this was the crucial point—it had nothing inside it. He put this intact but meatless shrimp on the table, next to the neat row formed by the other five—equally hollow—crustaceans. Again, a string of exclamations came from the three girls.

Just six months later, Lü Yuan became Horsie's wife. The other girls at the dinner got married too, to guys we didn't know.

.   .   .

BY MARRYING HORSIE, Lü Yuan detached him from us. From then on, when we sat down to a meal together, we were no longer joined by the avid diner. To be honest, we couldn't quite get used to it. We had begun to appreciate how striking were those two parallel lines across from us, Horsie's head and the tabletop—the unchanging distance between Horsie's head and the table surface so like that between a boarding jetty and the shore. Sometimes, when Horsie sat by the window and sunlight shone in from outside, we noticed that Horsie's head had a twin on the table's surface: a black shadow, slightly flattened at its extremities, which slowly shrunk to the thinnest of strips as the light shifted. We had never seen such a long and thin head, not even in a cartoon. Another time we were sitting in a dimly lit room and once, when I stood up, I bumped into the low-hanging ceiling lamp. The top of my head stung with a scorching pain, and the lamp itself swayed so violently that the shadow of Horsie's head swung to and fro on the table in crazy motion for a good two minutes, performing in that time practically all the headshaking Horsie would ever need to do.

After Horsie got married, Guo Bin was the only one of us who stayed in touch with him on a regular basis. Often, in the early evening, wearing a gray windbreaker, his hands in his pockets, he would walk from one end to the other of the longest street in town and arrive outside Horsie's apartment. Then he would curl his long fingers and knock on the door.

Guo Bin told his friends that the atmosphere in Horsie's new home was entirely Lü Yuan's creation. From the bedroom to the living room, the walls were crowded with close-ups of Lü Yuan. The earliest photo had been taken when she was just one month old and the others dated from each of the succeeding years, for a current total of twenty-three. In only three of the prints could one see Horsie's smile, and next to it was the more enchanting face of Lü Yuan. "Unless you look carefully," Guo Bin said, "you won't notice Horsie at all."

Guo Bin went on to tell us that the furniture in Horsie's house followed a white theme, decorated with pink highlights. The carpet was beige, the walls were beige, and even Horsie's clothes—the clothes purchased after he was married—had beige as the keynote. Guo Bin attributed all of this to Lü Yuan's preferences and recommendations. "Did you ever see Horsie wear beige before?" Guo Bin asked.

"Absolutely not." He answered his own question right away. "Now that Horsie dresses in beige," he went on, "he looks heavier than before, paler too."

Guo Bin said that Horsie's apartment was like a single girl's dorm room, with all kinds of knickknacks displayed: "From the bookshelves to the cabinets, there's little animals everywhere: flannel, glass, bamboo—you name it. There's even a big black flannel bear on top of the bed. But as for Horsie's things, you won't see so much as a pen of his on the table. It's only when his clothes are drying on the balcony that you have a chance of finding some trace of his property in the apartment." Guo Bin gave a smirk at the thought of the stuffed bear. "Could it be that even as a married woman," he asked us—and himself too—"Lü Yuan still hugs her bear when she goes to sleep?"

As time went on, Guo Bin's familiarity with Horsie's apartment grew steadily more complete, and he would brag that even if he were to walk around the apartment for half an hour with his eyes closed he could still manage to avoid knocking into a single chair. What's more, he said he knew how items were distributed and what things could be found in what cabinet, and if anyone was curious he could provide a detailed inventory.

"There's a drawer in their bedside table," he said, "which holds all their identity papers and their bankbooks. It's locked. Under the drawer is a pile of Lü Yuan's panties and bras. There are stockings and scarves there too."

As for Horsie's underwear, socks, and scarves, there was no special place reserved for them, for they were crammed into a wardrobe with the rest of his stuff—winter clothes, summer clothes, spring and autumn clothes—all in a single drawer, no less. One time, Guo Bin saw for himself the immense effort involved if Horsie wanted to put his hands on a simple undershirt. It was as though he were searching through a garbage heap for discarded clothes, first sticking his head into the wardrobe, then his shoulders too, eventually emerging with just a pair of underpants in his hand. He tossed them aside, then took his entire collection of clothes in his arms and dumped everything on the floor. He knelt in front of this little mountain of clothing and spent another half hour rummaging around before at last he managed to find his undershirt.

Guo Bin gave us to understand that only he could grasp the subtle relations between Horsie and Lü Yuan. "You people just can't imagine what goes on between them." He gave an example to back up his claim.

Guo Bin was sitting in a chair when he began to tell us his story. He stood up, walked around in a little circle, and then looked at his three friends. Two days earlier, he said, he was about to knock on the door of Horsie's apartment when he heard the sound of sobbing inside—low but prolonged sobs that he felt could only have been triggered by some heartrending sorrow. So he let his hand drop to his side and stood outside Horsie's door until the sobs subsided, until he could not hear them anymore. All this time he wondered why Lü Yuan was crying. What could have made her so sad? Had Horsie been mistreating her? But he hadn't heard Horsie yelling at her—in fact, he hadn't heard any talking at all.

After the sobbing had ceased, Guo Bin reckoned that Lü Yuan must now have dried her tears, so he raised his hand once again and knocked on the door. It was Horsie who opened up, and what astonished Guo Bin was that Horsie's eyes were wet, while Lü Yuan was sitting comfortably on the sofa with the TV remote in her hand. It was only then he realized the person who had just been crying was not Lü Yuan, but Horsie.

"Do you get it?" Guo Bin asked his friends, a smile on his lips. Then he went back to his chair and sat down, very much at ease.

ON THIS PARTICULAR DAY, that's to say the afternoon of June 30, 1996, Horsie stopped by Guo Bin's apartment. His wife, Lü Yuan, had left for Shanghai the previous day and wouldn't be back for a week, so Horsie, being all alone, thought of Guo Bin, because Guo Bin had an extensive collection of videos and Horsie wanted to borrow a few to watch at home and enliven this period of enforced bachelorhood.

Guo Bin had been having a nap. Wearing only a pair of jockey shorts, he opened the door and gave a long yawn. "Did Lü Yuan get off okay?" he asked, his eyes puffy from sleep.

Horsie was a bit taken aback. He wondered how Guo Bin knew Lü Yuan was out of town. "How did you know she's away?" he asked.

Guo Bin rubbed his eyes. "You told me she had a trip planned."

"When was that?" Horsie didn't remember this at all.

"Then it must have been Lü Yuan."

As Guo Bin said this, he went into the toilet and had a pee, not bothering to close the door. Horsie sat on the sofa and watched as Guo Bin gave another yawn, rubbing his eyes again with one hand and tugging the toilet chain with the other. Amid the din of the flushing water, Guo Bin came out of the bathroom and shuffled over to the sofa. He hesitated a moment, then turned around and lay back down in bed.

Horsie noticed a camcorder in the corner by the balcony. "Whose camera is that?" he asked.

"It's mine," Guo Bin said. "I bought it last month."

Horsie nodded. "I'd like to borrow a few videos," he said.

"What kind do you want? Action or romance?"

Horsie thought about this. "Both."

"Help yourself," Guo Bin said.

He told Horsie the thrillers were on the third and fourth shelves and the love stories on the fifth shelf and the right-hand side of the sixth shelf. Guo Bin rubbed away gum from his eyes and yawned.

Horsie walked over to the bookcase and scanned its contents. He took out two tapes, one from the third shelf and one from the fifth. When he turned around, Guo Bin seemed to have drifted off to sleep. He hesitated a moment, then said quietly, "I'm taking two tapes."

Guo Bin opened his eyes. He propped himself up and his head tilted in Horsie's direction. "Go back to sleep," Horsie said. "I'm off now."

A smile appeared on Guo Bin's face, an odd kind of smile. "How about something erotic?" he asked.

Horsie smiled too. Guo Bin jumped out of bed, knelt on the floor, and pulled a carton out from underneath the bed. When he opened the box, Horsie could see it was filled halfway with videos. "All porn," Guo Bin said proudly. "Is it Hong Kong and Taiwan movies you want?" he asked. "Or foreign?"

"I don't know."

Guo Bin stood up. Seeing Horsie at a loss to know what to choose, he patted him on the shoulder. "Just pick one," he said, "any one you like."

Horsie chose one at random. In bed that evening, he first watched a love story that moved him to tears and then watched a thriller that made his hair stand on end. He reserved the porn movie for the finale.

Horsie inserted the video into the warm VCR and went to the bathroom as the tape rewound. By the time he came out, the tape had begun to play. He saw a mass of snowflakes, and after a few moments a picture appeared on the screen: a naked woman lying on her back, her head buried in a pillow, her legs together. A man's arm moved on the left side of the frame; shoulders appeared, then the man's back. The man walked toward the bed, put a hand on the mattress to steady himself, then clambered onto the bed. He separated the woman's legs and mounted her.

Horsie heard a little groan as the man began to move back and forth on the woman's body. He was struck by the way the man's buttocks trembled, as though shivering with cold. Horsie heard the man pant, and the woman too, then constant groaning from the woman. In the following frames there was no significant change, but the bodies clamped together on the bed swayed slightly; a quiver had seized them. This uneventful scene lasted a little longer, until two cries were heard. The bodies now lay glued together, motionless, as though dead. After a little while the man shifted his weight and detached himself from his partner. She gave a long, capricious moan. The man knelt on the bed, his back to the camera; he was doing something with his head lowered.

Horsie realized that their job was done, but . . . "Why wasn't there any music?" he wondered.

He thought this very strange. "Can it be that porn flicks don't have music?"

The man lay down once more, shoulder to shoulder with the woman. They linked feet and pulled a blanket over their naked bodies.

"How was it?" Horsie heard the man ask.

"Fantastic," the woman answered.

After a moment of silence he suddenly heard his own name spoken. "Am I better than Horsie, then?"

"Oh, no comparison."

Just as Horsie was wondering if he had imagined it, he heard his name once more. "What's Horsie like in bed?" the man asked.

"What a pain you are!" She gave him a little punch. "Didn't I tell you already?"

"I want to hear it again," the man said.

The woman laughed. "He doesn't move."

"What do you mean, he doesn't move?"

"You won't leave it alone, will you?" Another laugh.

The man persisted. "What do you mean he doesn't move?"

"Once he's in, he just doesn't move . . . You're such a pain." She gave him another punch.

"What does he do then?"

"He gets on top of me and lies there, not doing anything, just pressing down on me, so hard I can hardly breathe . . . Satisfied?" the woman asked.

"How long does he spend there on top of you, not doing anything?"

"It varies. There have been a few times when he fell asleep on top of me . . ."

"What do you do if he falls asleep?"

"I give a heave and push him off . . . Is that enough for you now?"

They burst out laughing. Then the man sat up. Turning toward the camera, he got out of bed. "Let's have a look at our recording," he said.

Horsie recognized the man who came forward. It was Guo Bin. Toward the back of the shot, the woman was now sitting up. Lü Yuan smiled at the camera.

A WEEK LATER, Lü Yuan returned home. As she pushed open the door, she could see Horsie eating his dinner at the table by the balcony. Lü Yuan observed, needless to say, those familiar parallel lines; a bowl of noodles had flushed Horsie's face to a deep red. She tossed her handbag onto the sofa. "Go fetch my suitcase," she said.

Horsie raised his head and cast her a glance, then resumed dining. Lü Yuan went into the kitchen, turned on the faucet, and splashed water on her face. She patted her face lightly with the palm of her hand, took some cream from the rack, and massaged her cheeks. When she returned to the living room, Horsie was still meticulously attending to his meal. She looked around. "Where's my suitcase?" she asked.

Horsie carried on as before, not bothering to look up. "Where's my suitcase?" Lü Yuan repeated.

Still no answer. Lü Yuan's voice rose several registers. "Get downstairs now!" she practically bellowed.

Horsie looked up and pulled a tissue from the box on the table. He delicately wiped his mouth. "Why did you say I don't move?" he asked.

Lü Yuan, having lost her temper, was quite unprepared for this sort of question and did not take it in at all. "Go fetch my suitcase!" she yelled again.

Horsie persisted. "Why did you say I don't move?"

It began to dawn on Lü Yuan just what had happened. She stopped shouting and looked at Horsie very intently. He took another tissue and wiped the sweat from his face. "Actually I do move . . . ," he said.

Horsie paused. "At the critical moment, I do move."

So saying, Horsie lowered his head and attended to the last two mouthfuls of noodles. Lü Yuan quietly went into the bedroom, and after sitting on the bed for a while she quietly went downstairs and brought up the suitcase herself.

There was no further drama. My friend Horsie did not return the videos to Guo Bin, nor did Guo Bin ask for them back. In the weeks that followed, Guo Bin would sometimes, as before, walk the length of the longest street in town, wearing his gray windbreaker. Hands in his pockets, he would arrive outside Horsie's apartment, curl his long fingers, and knock on the door.

VICTORY

Lin Hong, tidying Li Hanlin's drawers, came upon an old envelope, neatly folded. When she opened it, she found another envelope inside, folded just as neatly. Inside this envelope she found another folded envelope, and in that she found a key.

It was an ordinary aluminum key, unremarkable in every way, so why would Li Hanlin store it inside three envelopes? Lin Hong studied the key in her hand and noticed that it was a little grimy: clearly it had been in use for quite some time. From its size she could tell the key would open not a door but a drawer or suitcase. She stood up, walked over to Li Hanlin's desk, and inserted the key into the keyhole of the drawer, but found that it failed to turn in the lock; next, she tried the keyholes of her suitcases and Li Hanlin's; and then she checked all the other locks in their apartment, but the key didn't open any of them. In other words, it had nothing to do with this home of theirs, which meant that . . . it was an interloper.

Lin Hong, a woman in her midthirties, was assailed by suspicion, disquiet, foreboding, and conjecture. Key in hand, she sat outside on the balcony, and for a long time she stayed there, unmoving; the sun above shifted its position above her stationary form. She felt lost. Only when the telephone rang did she rise and go inside to answer it. The call was from her husband, in a hotel far away. "Lin Hong, Li Hanlin here," he said. "I got here okay and checked in. Everything's fine. Are you okay?"

Was she okay? She didn't know. She stood there, receiver in

hand. The voice at the other end was saying, "Hello? Hello? Can you hear me?"

She said something at last. "I can hear you."

"Okay, I'll hang up now."

The connection was broken, and all that came over the line was a long silence. Lin Hong hung up and went back to the balcony to stare at the key. Her husband's call had been a routine formality, a simple confirmation that he was still alive.

That was one thing there was no doubt about. His clothes were drying on the balcony, his smile was mounted in a frame on the wall, cigarettes he had stubbed out were still lying in the ashtray, and his friends were calling on the phone, unaware he was away. "What?" they'd say. "Another business trip?"

She looked at the key. Her husband's entire existence seemed to hinge on it. But just what did this grubby key signify? Someone she had thought was so close to her had kept a secret from her, just as neatly and securely as those three envelopes had guarded the key, and this secret had been concealed by time, concealed by time that she had imagined to be happy. Now that secret was about to be revealed, and—she felt sure—it was going to do her damage. She heard footsteps coming up the stairs. Steadily they approached her door, paused, then continued the climb.

The following morning, Lin Hong went to Li Hanlin's office and told his office mate that she needed to pick up a few things from his desk drawer. The colleague knew her. Wives were always fetching things from their husbands' offices. He pointed to a desk by the window.

She inserted the key into the keyhole of Li Hanlin's desk, and the latch snapped open. And that was how she discovered her husband's secret, inside a large envelope. There were two photographs of the same woman, one of her in a swimsuit on a beach, the other a black-and-white portrait. She looked younger than Lin Hong, but not more attractive. Then there were five letters, all signed "Qingqing." The name made her eyes burn. Qingqing . . . this was obviously a pet name. For a woman who was completely unknown to her to share a pet name with her husband . . . The hand that held the letters began to tremble. The letters were full of sweet sentiments and touching endearments. It seemed that this woman and Li Hanlin often met, and frequently chatted on the phone. That was the way it was. And there was no exhausting their sweet sentiments and touching endearments; letters had to be exchanged to allow more room for their expression. In one of the letters, the woman told Li Hanlin she had a new telephone number.

AFTER LIN HONG GOT HOME, she sat down on the sofa and studied this seven-digit number. She tried to collect herself, and then she picked up the phone and dialed. She heard ringing, and then a woman answered. "Hello?"

"I'd like to speak to Qingqing," Lin Hong said.

"Speaking. Who's calling?"

Lin Hong detected a husky quality to the woman's voice. "I'm the wife of Li Hanlin," she said.

For a long time there was no reply, but Lin Hong could hear breathing, uneven breathing. "You're shameless," Lin Hong said. "You're despicable, you sneaky little . . ." Lin Hong didn't know what to say next; her whole body was shaking.

The other party now spoke. "Tell it to Li Hanlin."

"You're shameless!" Lin Hong shouted into the phone. "You've destroyed our marriage!"

"I haven't destroyed your marriage," the other woman said. "Relax, I'm not going to do that. Li Hanlin and I won't go any further; this is our limit. I'm not interested in marrying him—not all women are like you." She hung up.

Lin Hong stood there, quivering from head to toe, as tears of indignation poured from her eyes and the dial tone rang in her ears. After a long time she put down the receiver, but she remained standing there, and then she picked up the phone again and dialed another number.

At the other end a male voice could be heard. "Hello? Hello? Who's calling? Why don't you say something?"

"This is Lin Hong."

"Oh, Lin Hong . . . Is Li Hanlin back now?"

"No."

"How come he's not back yet? It's been a while now, hasn't it? No, it can't be that long. I saw him three days ago. What's he doing this time? Is he still promoting that water filter? What a scam that is! He gave me one and I tried it out. I put filtered water in one glass and water from the faucet in another glass, and I couldn't see any difference between the two. Then I drank a mouthful from each glass and they tasted the same, too."

Lin Hong interrupted him. "Do you know Qingqing?"

"Qingqing?" he said. There was a pause. Lin Hong waited, holding the receiver. "I don't know her," he said finally.

Lin Hong tried to stay calm. "Li Hanlin is having an affair. He's hooked up with some woman behind my back. Her name is Qingqing. I just found out today. They meet, they talk on the phone, they write to each other. I have the letters she sent him. They've known each other for more than a year now—"

This time it was the man at the other end who interrupted her. "I know Li Hanlin pretty well," he said, "but I don't know anything about this Qingqing person. Could you have misinterpreted? Perhaps they're just friends . . . Excuse me, someone's knocking at the door. Hold on."

He put down the phone, and after a moment she heard two men talking and steps coming toward the telephone. The receiver was picked up and the man said, "Hello?"

She knew that he was waiting for her to go on, but she didn't want to say more, so all she said was "If you have a guest, I'll let you go."

"Okay, we'll talk about it later."

He hung up. Lin Hong still clutched the receiver. She looked up the number of another friend of Li Hanlin. She dialed and heard someone pick up the phone. "Hello?"

"This is Lin Hong," she said.

"Lin Hong, how are you? And how's Li Hanlin? What's he up to these days?"

She was quiet for a moment. "Do you know Qingqing?"

There was a long silence at the other end of the line. She had no choice but to continue. "Li Hanlin has been carrying on with another woman behind my back."

"Surely not." Now, at last, he spoke. "Li Hanlin wouldn't do that kind of thing. I know him. Is it possible that you're being a bit . . . over-suspicious?"

"I've got evidence," Lin Hong said. "I've got the letters this woman wrote, and the photos she gave him. I called her up on the phone just now, also."

"I don't know anything about this."

His tone was frosty, and Lin Hong knew she would get nothing more out of him, so she hung up the phone and went to the balcony and sat down. Li Hanlin had a few other friends, but she didn't want to call them. They would simply come to his defense and show her no sympathy. A long time ago she had had friends of her own—Zhao Ping, Zhang Lini, and Shen Ning—but she had drifted apart from them after her marriage, hanging out with Li Hanlin's pals, chatting and joking with them, going shopping with their wives. Those wives had replaced Zhao Ping, Zhang Lini, and Shen Ning. Only now did she realize she had lost all her friends.

She had no idea how to get in touch with Zhao Ping or Zhang Lini. She had only Shen Ning's number, scribbled down a year ago when they had run into each other in the street. She had written the number in her book and then forgotten all about it.

It was Shen Ning's husband who answered the phone. He told Lin Hong to hang on, and then Shen Ning came on the line. "Yes, who is it?"

"It's me, Lin Hong."

She heard a yelp of delight at the other end, then Shen Ning unleashed a stream of comments and questions: "It's great to hear your voice! I called you once, but nobody picked up. Are you doing well? It's been ages since we saw each other. A year now, right? It seems like ages. Have you heard from Zhao Ping and Zhang Lini at all? It's been years since I saw them, too. Are you doing well?"

"No, I'm not doing well," Lin Hong said.

Shen Ning went quiet. "What did you say?"

Tears began to spill from Lin Hong's eyes. "My husband has been cheating on me. He's been carrying on with some woman . . ." She was sobbing too much to continue.

"What happened?" Shen Ning asked.

"Yesterday," Lin Hong said, "yesterday, when I was tidying his drawer, I found a folded envelope, and when I opened it I found two more envelopes inside. He had hidden a key inside those three envelopes. I got suspicious and tried all the locks in the apartment, but it didn't open any of them. So I thought maybe it was the key to his office desk, and this morning I went to his office, and that's where I found the letters that this woman wrote to him, as well as a couple of photos—"

"Outrageous!" Shen Ning started cursing.

Now that Lin Hong had an ally at last, her grief and resentment could find release. "I did everything for him," she said. "I never gave a moment's thought to whether there were things I should have. All the time I was thinking of what I could do for him, what he'd like to eat, what clothes he should wear. After we got married, I completely forgot about myself. All that mattered to me was catering to his needs, and now look what he gets up to . . ."

"What's your plan?" Shen Ning asked.

"I don't know."

"I'll tell you," Shen Ning said. "You can't afford to be weak at this point, and you can't be softhearted, either. You have to punish him. No more crying from now on—whatever you do, don't let him see you cry. You need to look furious and ignore him. Don't cook his meals; don't do his laundry; don't do anything for him. Don't let him sleep in your bed—make him sleep on the sofa. At the very least, make him sleep on the sofa for a year or so. He'll beg you, he'll get down on his knees, he'll even slap himself on the face, but stick to your guns. He'll make all kinds of promises—men are good at that, but their promises are worth no more than a dog's bark. Don't believe a word of it. In short, you need to make him understand the costs incurred when he has a romantic adventure, you have to give him a taste of hell on earth, you have to make him feel that life's not worth living, that he'd be better off dead."

A FEW DAYS LATER, Li Hanlin came back from his trip. He found Lin Hong sitting on the balcony, indifferent to his homecoming. He laid his bag on the sofa, went over to Lin Hong, and looked at her. She seemed to have been struck dumb. "What's wrong?" he said.

Lin Hong's eyes were fixed on the floor. Li Hanlin waited by her side, and when she still said nothing he went over to the sofa, opened his bag, and dumped out the dirty clothes, then looked at her. He was displeased to find her still staring at the floor. "What's the meaning of this?" he said.

Lin Hong turned away from him and surveyed the view from the balcony. Li Hanlin went back to rummaging around in his bag. He took out his other belongings and laid them on the sofa. Then he began to lose his temper. He walked over to Lin Hong and started to shout. "What the hell is this about? I come home and you put on a sourpuss face. What have I done to offend you now? You—"

He could see that Li Hanlin stopped abruptly. A key was clasped between Lin Hong's finger and thumb. There was a buzzing noise in his head. He stood there a moment, then went to his study and opened a drawer. Some magazines were stacked inside. He groped around underneath the magazines, but failed to find the neatly folded envelope in the right-hand corner. He realized he was breathing heavily.

Li Hanlin stood by the window for a long time. Then he left the room and walked quietly over to Lin Hong. He bent down. "You've been to my office?"

Lin Hong sat there motionless. Li Hanlin looked at her. "You've read Qingqing's letters?"

Lin Hong began to tremble. Li Hanlin hesitated, then put his hand on her shoulder. Lin Hong jerked violently, knocking his hand away. It returned to its original position and hung there for a moment before he put it in his trouser pocket. "This is the situation," he said. "I met Qingqing two years ago, at a friend's house. She's a cousin of his, so she often stops by. One day I ran into her in the street and we began seeing each other. She lives with her parents and I live with you, so we're not in a position . . . What I mean to say is, she and I are not in a position to have sex. When we meet, it's in a cinema or a park or just walking in the street. She and I, all we've done is . . . all we've done is kiss."

Lin Hong was weeping now. The hand came out of the pocket and reached for her shoulder, but it retreated when her shoulder shrank back. Li Hanlin rubbed his forehead. "That's the sum total of my interaction with her. Even if you hadn't found out, she and I wouldn't have gone any further. Our marriage is very precious to me. I would never break up this home of ours."

Lin Hong sprang to her feet, strode into the bedroom, and slammed the door. Li Hanlin didn't move. After several minutes, he walked over to the bedroom and tapped lightly on the door. "I won't see Qingqing anymore," he said.

LIN HONG THOUGHT, he didn't beg me to forgive him, he didn't fall on his knees, he didn't slap himself in the face, he didn't pledge oaths, and he didn't even apologize.

He did sleep on the sofa, however. Shen Ning was right on that score, at least. He had lingered by her bedside, standing there like a businessman weighing the pros and cons, and finally he had opted for the sofa.

By opting for the sofa, he had opted for silence, opted for a life where he and she lived separately.

Now that his life and hers had parted ways, he said nothing further on the topic of Qingqing, and naturally he no longer acted as a husband would. He was careful and circumspect. As he moved about the apartment he did his best to make no noise, and he did not turn on the television. He limited his activities to the sofa, where he either sat or lay, reading. He never used to read at all, but now he always had a book in his hand.

Whenever she appeared, he would put down the book he was reading and look at her, partly to get some sense of her state of mind, partly to make his own position clear: he had not lost himself in the pleasures of reading; he was still fidgeting uneasily in the real world.

His silence infuriated her. Did he think that by eliminating all sound from their home, he could muddle his way through the crisis? It wouldn't work, because she wouldn't stand for it— she wouldn't allow him to have a quiet life. He had betrayed her, and now he thought he could make up for it by pussyfooting around?

She began to provoke him. Seeing him sitting on the sofa, with his feet on the floor, she walked toward the balcony, giving his feet a kick as she passed, as though they were blocking her way. She went out onto the balcony and waited for him to react, but he didn't. Not even pain could force him to make a sound. There was nothing for it but to return to the bedroom. This time she noticed that he had now withdrawn his feet and put them on the sofa.

She persisted with her provocations. In the early evening she walked over to the sofa and dumped his bedding, clothes, and books on the floor, then sat down and turned on the television.

He just sat there on the sofa as she cleared away his things, but once the TV was on he stood up and went out to the balcony. He sat on the floor of the balcony and read his book. He did this to demonstrate his modesty, his belief that he didn't deserve to sit next to her, didn't deserve to watch television with her. He continued to sit on the hard balcony floor, getting up from time to time to stretch, then sitting back down. Only after she had returned to the bedroom did he go back to the sofa, reclaim the items she had flung on the floor, and lie down to sleep.

His boundless silence left her at a loss. All her provocations were like stones cast into the ocean.

The next night, she abandoned the bed and lay down on the sofa to watch television. She fell asleep there with the TV on and didn't wake up until morning. This was part of her scheme, but it seemed natural as well. She had occupied his sleeping area, and at the same time conceded her bed to him, expecting the soft bed to entice him and lull him into unwary slumber, thus giving her an opportunity to engage in further hostilities.

But when she woke up on the sofa, she found him sitting on a chair, his head cushioned on the dining table, fast asleep.

He was going around the house with his tail tucked between his legs, as though he were punishing himself. The problem was that this kind of punishment punished her as well. She couldn't shed the tears she wanted to shed, couldn't yell the things she wanted to yell. A fiery rage consumed her, but it could only smolder in her heart. By now she was no longer waiting for him to fall to his knees and beg her forgiveness: she had given up hope of getting the reaction that Shen Ning had predicted. What she wanted now was a huge row. Even if they came to blows, it would be better than this.

But he refused to provide her with this opportunity: that is, he rejected the punishment she had selected for him. He passed judgment on himself and punctiliously submitted to this judgment, making her feel, in the end, that he was now quite comfortably reconciled to his life of deprivation. Each morning he would leave before she did, and in the evening return from work after her. There was really no bone to pick here. He had a much longer commute than she did, and he had always left early and come home late. He ate lunch at his office, she knew, but where he was eating dinner in the evening she had no clue. When he came home at the end of the day, he didn't go into the kitchen, didn't even glance in that direction, so she knew he must already have eaten. He sat on the sofa and picked up a book. He had disrupted her life, thrown her into turmoil, but he had adjusted perfectly.

One evening, she was standing on the balcony when she caught sight of him coming out of a restaurant below, and it suddenly became clear where he had been eating his dinners. She was so angry she began to shake. For her, every day seemed like a year, but there he was, in and out of restaurants, treating himself to a life of luxury. She marched downstairs. She had already eaten, but she wasn't going to let that stop her from stuffing herself again. When they passed each other on the landing, she marched straight by him without looking his way and continued down the stairs and into the restaurant he had just left. She ordered several dishes and some wine, but could not stomach more than a couple of mouthfuls.

After three meals in the restaurant, she began to feel distressed about all the money she was spending. She was making inroads into their savings. They didn't have a lot of money in the first place, and there were plenty of basic things they still needed. Indignation, however, impelled her back to the restaurant, until the day that they happened to be there at the same time. She saw him as soon as she walked in, huddled over a bowl of noodles. She sat down at a distant table and watched the other people enjoying their extravagant meals, while he ate his wretched noodles. Suddenly she felt heartsick.

The next day, while cooking her dinner, she prepared a serving for him, too. She placed an empty bowl on the most conspicuous spot on the dining table, and a pair of chopsticks on top of the bowl, and the food she'd made beside it. She hoped he would notice as soon as he came in, and in this he did not disappoint her. His eyes lit up right away, and then he looked at her quizzically to confirm that the dinner was intended for him. Even though he'd already had his noodles, he sat down at the table and consumed the entire meal she had cooked.

By the time he had finished, she had gone into the bedroom and closed the door behind her. She lay on the bed and listened as he opened the door and walked over to her. After standing there for a while, he sat down on the edge of the bed. "Can we talk?" he asked.

She did not say anything. After a moment, he asked again, "Can we talk?"

Still she said nothing, hoping that a torrent of words would flood from his lips. In her view, he needed to take himself to task. Even if he didn't burst into tears, he should at least beat his breast and stamp his feet; he should get down on his knees the way Shen Ning had said he would; he should pledge solemn vows, he should say everything she wanted to hear. She would ignore him just the same, but these were things he had to do. Instead, all he could say was "Can we talk?"

He sat on her bed for a long time, but when she made no reply he stood up and left. After he had gently closed the door behind him, she began to weep. How could he just slip out like that, so nonchalantly?

He went back to the sofa, and after he lay down the progress that had been made was nullified; they were back where they had started.

AFTER TWENTY-SIX DAYS OF THIS, Li Hanlin finally couldn't take it anymore. He told Lin Hong that he had a constant ache in every joint, an agonizing crick in his neck, and a chronic stomachache as well. "We can't go on like this," he said.

Now, at last, he was speaking assertively. He was circumspect no more. He stood gesticulating before Lin Hong, the image of self-assurance. "I have already punished myself," he said, "and still you won't forgive me. If we carry on like this, I won't be the only one to suffer—you'll find it equally unbearable. I really have had more than I can take. I just can't go on like this anymore. The only thing to do is . . ." He paused for a moment. "The only thing to do is get divorced."

As he spoke, Lin Hong had her back to him, but when he said this she spun around. "Forget about divorcing me! You hurt me, and you still haven't paid the price. You want to high-tail it out of here. You want to run off to your Qingqing, but I won't have it. I am going to pin you down, pin you down till you're old, pin you down till you're dead."

When a smile appeared on Li Hanlin's face, she suddenly understood. He wasn't at all opposed to being pinned down, being pinned down until his hair had gone white, until he was dead. He wouldn't raise the slightest objection. So she broke off and stood there, unsure what to do. She felt tears falling, and this simply added to her humiliation. So many days of misery, and a smile was all she got. For weeks she had been waiting for his repentance, his self-indictment. At the very least, he should shed some heartfelt tears, demonstrate true remorse, but he wasn't doing anything like that; instead, he was standing in front of her, declaring boldly, "The only thing to do is get divorced."

She raised her hand and wiped her tears away. "All right, forget it," she said. "Better to get divorced."

At this, his smile vanished. She went into the bedroom, locked the door, lay down on the bed, and fell asleep with her clothes on.

THEY WERE WALKING TOWARD the registry office. That was where they had gone to formalize their marriage, and now they were going to dissolve it. A wall ran along one side of the street and Li Hanlin walked in front, Lin Hong a few steps behind. From time to time he would stop and wait for her to catch up, then walk on. Neither of them said a word. Li Hanlin bowed his head and knitted his brows, as though weighed down by worry. Lin Hong walked with her head up, letting the autumn breeze toss her hair about. Now and again, a wisp of a smile could be seen on her otherwise expressionless face. It was a smile like a falling leaf, desolate, lifeless.

They passed shops they used to frequent and bus stops where they had waited together. As they walked on and on, it seemed as though time were running backward. When Li Hanlin reached a coffee shop called Sundown, he came to a halt and waited for Lin Hong. He stopped because he'd remembered that they had come here right after registering their marriage: they had sat by a window overlooking the street, and he had ordered a cup of coffee and she a Sprite. "Shall we go in and have a drink?" he called.

By now Lin Hong had caught up with him. She turned, looked upward, and saw a neon sign above the eaves, the tubes of light forming the words "Sundown Café." She agreed to his suggestion and together they entered. It was afternoon, and customers were few. They selected a table by the window, overlooking the street, and once again he ordered a coffee and she a Sprite. They thought about what they had drunk that earlier time.

Li Hanlin was the first to smile, followed soon by Lin Hong, but they quickly suppressed their smiles and avoided each other's eyes. He looked out the window, and she looked at the other people in the coffee shop. She noticed a young woman dressed in red, sitting alone on their right. The woman was

watching them. It seemed to Lin Hong that she had a strange
look on her face. Lin Hong put two and two together, and a
name flashed into her head: Qingqing.

Lin Hong threw Li Hanlin a glance. He, too, had seen the
woman. From the surprised look on his face, it was clear he
had not expected to run into her here. When he turned his
head, he found Lin Hong's eyes on him, and he knew that she
knew. He gave a wry smile.

"So you told her," Lin Hong said.

"What?"

"You told her we were going to get divorced, so she came
here."

"No."

Lin Hong felt her heart flood with pain. "You needn't have
been in such a rush."

"No," he said again. "She doesn't know anything."

She looked at him intently. He had such a firm expression
on his face that she began to give some credence to what he'd
said. She looked back at the young woman. This Qingqing was
watching them, but as soon as Lin Hong glanced at her she
turned away. "She's staring at you," Lin Hong said. "You'd better go over and say hello."

"No," he said.

"We're about to get divorced. What are you worried about?"

"No," he repeated.

She looked at him. His unshakeable attitude suddenly gave
her a warm feeling. She took another peek at Qingqing. This
time she wasn't looking at them; she was drinking from her
glass. One leg was perched on top of the other. In her posture,
she seemed to lack the composure one might have expected.

Lin Hong took another look at Li Hanlin, who was staring grimly out the window. "Kiss me," she said.

He turned around in astonishment.

"Kiss me," she repeated. "After this, you'll never kiss me again, so I want you to kiss me now."

He nodded and reached across the table.

"Sit next to me when you kiss me," she said.

So he stood up and sat down next to her and pressed his lips to her cheek.

"Put your arms around me," she said.

He put his arms around her, and he felt her lips brushing over his face and meeting his lips. Her tongue slipped into his mouth, and her arms embraced him. It seemed to him a kiss as long as night. She used her hands to hold his body in place and her tongue to keep his mouth in place. Her ardor entered his body through his mouth, spreading and expanding boundlessly.

Through it all, Lin Hong's eyes were fixed on the other woman. She watched as Qingqing kept glancing in their direction, as she uneasily fingered her glass, and as, in the end, she stood up and hurried out. When her red silhouette slipped past them, Lin Hong's heart filled with joy, for she had the sudden conviction that victory was hers. After twenty-seven days of grief and indignation, insomnia and emptiness, her enemy had surrendered without a fight.

Her hands slipped off Li Hanlin's body, and her mouth disengaged from his. She turned to him with a smile.

Appendix

My father used to be a surgeon. He was a strong, robust man with a resonant voice. He regularly stood at the operating table for ten hours at a time, but at the end of his shift his face would not show the slightest signs of fatigue, and as he walked back to our apartment his steps were loud and firm. Nearing home, he would often take a pee by the corner of the alley outside. His urine would splash noisily on the wall, like a sudden downpour of rain.

When my father was twenty-five years old, he married a pretty young worker from the textile mill, and in their second year of marriage she gave him a son, my older brother, and two years later she had another son, who was me.

When I was eight, the vigorous surgeon happened to get a day off from his usual hectic schedule. He enjoyed the luxury of sleeping all morning at home, and in the afternoon he went for a long walk with his sons and played with them on the beach for hours. On the way home he let one ride on his shoulders and carried the other in his arms. By the time they had finished dinner it was already dark, and he, his wife, and their two children sat underneath the parasol tree that stood outside their door. At that hour the moonlight shone down, casting the leaves' mottled shadows over us, and a cool breeze rustled.

The surgeon lay on a makeshift bamboo lounge chair, his wife sat in an adjacent rattan chair, and my brother and I sat next to each other on a bench. We listened as our father explained how everyone had an appendix in their belly and how every day he had to remove, at the very least, twenty or so appendixes. His fastest time was just fifteen minutes—fifteen minutes to perform the operation and cut off the appendix. We asked him what he did with it afterward.

"Afterward ..." my father waved his hand dismissively. "Afterward we throw it away."

"Why's that?"

"An appendix isn't worth a fart," he answered.

Then he had a question for us. "What are the lungs for?"

"For breathing in," my brother replied.

"What else?"

My brother thought for a moment: "And breathing out."

"And the tummy? What's the tummy for?"

"The tummy? The tummy digests things you have eaten." Again it was my brother who answered.

"And the heart?"

This time I beat him to it. "The heart beats, thump thump!"

My father glanced at me. "That's true, you're both right. The lungs, the stomach, the heart, as well as the duodenum, the colon, the large intestine, the rectum, and whatnot—they all have their various functions. It's just the appendix, the appendix at the end of the cecum ... Do you know what the appendix is good for?"

My brother had the answer ready. "The appendix isn't worth a fart."

My father laughed and our mother, sitting next to him, laughed too. "That's right," my father continued, "the appendix isn't good for anything. When you breathe, when you digest your meals, when you're sleeping, none of these activities involves the appendix in the slightest. Even when you eat so much that you burp or have a tummyache and give a fart, this doesn't have anything to do with your appendix either."

My brother and I tittered when we heard our father talking about burping and farting. Then he sat up. "But if the appendix gets inflamed," he told us gravely, "the tummy will ache more and more, and if the appendix is perforated it will cause peritonitis, and that can be fatal. Fatal, you understand what that means?"

My brother nodded. "It'll kill you."

I gasped when I heard that. Seeing my reaction, my father patted me on the head. "Actually, removal of the appendix is a minor procedure," he said. "So long as there's no perforation, there's no danger . . . There was a British surgeon . . ."

As my father spoke, he lay back in his chair. We knew he was going to tell a story. He closed his eyes and gave a contented yawn, then turned to face us. He said that one day the British surgeon arrived on a little island. This little island had no hospital and no doctor and not even a medical kit, but his appendix became inflamed and he lay underneath a palm tree, racked with pain for a whole morning. He knew if there was any further delay in operating, his appendix would perforate . . .

"And what happens if the appendix perforates?" My father propped himself up.

"He'll be a goner," my brother said.

"It will turn into peritonitis, and then he'll be a goner," my father corrected him.

"The British surgeon had no choice but to operate on himself," he went on. "He had two natives hold up a big mirror and, looking at himself in the mirror, in this particular spot . . ."

My father pointed at the right side of his stomach. "In this very spot he made an incision in the skin, pushed the fat aside, put his hand in, searched for the cecum—you need to find that first before you can find the appendix . . ."

A British surgeon operating on himself: this incredible story left us spellbound. We looked at our father, our eyes gleaming, and asked him if he could operate on himself too, just like the British surgeon.

"That depends on the situation," he said. "If I was on that little island and my appendix was inflamed, to save my own life I would operate on myself too."

Father's reply made the blood flow hot in our veins. We had always thought him to be the strongest, most capable man in the world, and his answer further confirmed us in this belief. It also gave us the confidence to brag to the other boys. "Our Dad operates on himself," I would say. "The two of us hold up a big mirror," my brother would add, pointing at me.

That's how the next couple of months passed. In the autumn of that year, our father's appendix became inflamed. It was a Sunday morning. Our mother was about to go off to the factory to put in some overtime when our father returned from the night shift. He came in the door just as she was leaving. "I didn't get any sleep at all last night," he said. "There was a head injury, two fractures, and a penicillin toxicosis. I'm so worn out, my body's aching."

Patting his chest, he lay down on his bed to sleep. My brother and I were in the other room. We put the table on top of the chairs, and then put the chairs on top of the table; three or four hours passed as we moved the furniture around this way and that. When we heard our father groaning in his room, we went over and put our ears to the door. After a moment we realized he was calling our names, so we pushed the door open and went in. We found him curled up like a shrimp, looking at us with clenched teeth. "My appendix . . . ," he said. "Ahhh! . . . it's killing me . . . acute appendicitis. Hurry up and go to the hospital. Ask for Dr. Chen . . . or Dr. Wang would do . . . quickly, go . . ."

My brother grabbed me by the hand and we went downstairs, out the door, and along the alley. Now I realized what was happening. Father's appendix was inflamed, and we were going to the hospital to fetch Dr. Chen or Dr. Wang. Once we'd found them, what would they do?

When I thought of Father's appendix all inflamed, my heart pounded. I thought to myself: So, at last, Father's appendix is inflamed. Now he can operate on himself, and my brother and I can hold up the big mirror.

My brother stopped when we reached the end of the alley. "We can't go and fetch Dr. Chen, nor Dr. Wang either."

"Why not?" I said.

"Well, look, if we find them, they'll do an operation."

I nodded. "Don't you want to see Dad operate on himself?" my brother asked.

"Yes, that *is* what I want," I said.

"So we can't look for Dr. Chen or Dr. Wang. We'll go to the operating theater and nab a surgical kit. As for the big mirror, we have one of those at home . . ."

I was so happy I shouted. "Yes! This way we can let Dad do the operation himself."

When we got to the hospital, practically all the staff was having lunch in the cafeteria and there was just one nurse in the operating theater. My brother told me to chat her up, so I went over and called her Auntie and asked her how she could possibly be so pretty. As she smiled and simpered, my brother stole a surgical kit.

Then we went back home. Father heard us come in. "Dr. Chen, Dr. Chen! Is that you, Dr. Wang?" he called in a low voice.

We went into his room. Father's forehead was bathed in sweat. The pain was getting to him. He could see there was no Dr. Chen, and no Dr. Wang either, just his two sons, my brother and me. "What about Dr. Chen? Why isn't Dr. Chen here?" he asked hoarsely.

My brother told me to open the surgical kit, while he brought over the big mirror our mother used to check her outfit each morning. Father didn't know what we were up to. "And Dr. Wang?" he asked. "Dr. Wang wasn't there either?"

We laid out the surgical kit on Father's right. I clambered on top of the bed and together we lifted up the mirror. My brother made a point of leaning forward and taking a peek in the mirror, to check that Father could see himself clearly. "Dad, get on with it!" we said excitedly.

By now he was in such pain, his features were contorted. Gasping, he stared at us, still peppering us with questions about Dr. Chen and Dr. Wang. We were getting desperate. "Dad, hurry up," we cried. "Otherwise it will get perforated!"

"Hurry up . . . with what?" he asked, weakly.

"Dad, hurry up and operate!" we said.

Now, finally, he understood. He glared at us. "You bastards!" he cursed.

I was shocked, not knowing what we'd done wrong, and

looked inquiringly at my brother, who was equally taken aback. Father was in such agony he couldn't speak, and he stared at us in silence. Returning his gaze, my brother realized at last why Father had cursed us. "We haven't taken Dad's pants off yet," he said.

My brother had me hold the mirror while he tried to pull down Dad's pants, but our father slapped him across the face and, straining with effort, cursed us again. "Bastards!"

This frightened my brother so much that he scurried off the bed, and I followed suit, quickly crawling over Dad's legs and onto the floor. We stood there side by side, looking at him as he lay there in a powerless rage. "Can it be Dad doesn't want to do the operation?" I asked.

"I don't know."

Tears welled up in our father's eyes. "Be good boys," he moaned, struggling to get his words out. "Hurry . . . hurry and fetch . . . Mom. Tell Mom to come . . ."

We'd been hoping Father would operate on himself like a hero, and now here he was, crying! We looked at him a moment longer, and then my brother took my hand and we ran out the door, down the stairs and along the full length of the alley. This time we didn't think up our own plan of action—we went to fetch Mom.

By the time our father was carried into the operating theater, his appendix was perforated and his stomach was filled with pus. He developed peritonitis and had to spend weeks and weeks in a hospital bed, and then convalesce at home for another month before he could again don a white smock and resume his job as doctor. But he could never again be a surgeon, for his energy was spent: if he were to stand at the operating table for an hour he would grow faint and his eyes would blur. He had gone thin overnight and never regained the weight he lost. When he walked, there was no longer that spring to his stride, and though he might take a big first step he would only go half as far with his second. When winter came, he seemed to have a constant cold. So from then on he could be only a doctor of internal medicine, and he would sit at a desk every day, chatting idly with the patients, scrawling routine prescriptions. After he got off work he would walk slowly homeward, rubbing his hands with a cotton ball soaked in alcohol. When we went to bed in the evenings, we would often hear him grumbling to our mother. "People think you have given me two sons, but appendixes are all they are. At the best of times they are of no worldly use, and when push comes to shove they are practically the death of you."

MID-AIR COLLISIONS

On an evening in August, the room was stifling hot. My wife and I were sitting in front of a rattling electric fan. I held the remote in my hand and changed the channels one by one, and then ran through them again in reverse sequence. My back was soaked in sweat and I was in an irritable mood. My wife, on the other hand, was quite composed, sitting there perfectly still. On her shiny forehead I couldn't see even a bead of sweat, and she seemed to be illustrating the old saying "Your body feels cool, mind calm as a pool." But I wasn't happy with things: since I'd got married, in fact, I had begun to be *unhappy* with things. Cursing under my breath, I banged away at the keys, converting the TV picture into a series of flashes, making my young eyes go blurry. I cursed the summer heat, the TV programs, the lousy rattling fan, the dinner I had just eaten, the underwear drying on the balcony . . . My wife kept her composure: so long as I was in this room, so long as I was keeping her company, then however much I cussed, whatever crazy thing I did, she would be perfectly at ease. If I were to walk out of this room, leave her and go off on my own, she would be singing a different tune. She would feel uneasy, she would be miserable; she would make a song-and-dance, all upset and tearful. That's marriage for you. I can never leave her for a second. That's my job as a husband, till ripe old age and death us do part.

My friend Morning Tang knocked on the door. He used his fingers, his fist, his feet, maybe even his knees—at any rate he made a hammering noise on the door. It was as though I heard a bugle call or a rooster crow, for I jumped up from the floor, opened the door, and saw before me Morning Tang, whom I hadn't seen in over a year. "Morning Tang, you rascal!" I cried.

Morning Tang was looking very dapper in baggy pants and a rust-colored jacket, but he had a funny smile on his face. He took a step forward, but stopped short. "Come on in," I said.

He entered cautiously, peering around the narrow hallway as if walking in such pitch-darkness he couldn't see his own fingers. I knew he was trying to establish my wife's whereabouts. It was because of her that he hadn't been to my house for over a year. In her words, Morning Tang is a jerk.

Actually, that's not true. Morning Tang is a good-hearted fellow, generous and kind to his friends, it's just there are too many women in his life, and that's why my wife said he was a jerk. In the past, he would often drop by with a woman in tow. Nothing wrong with that—the problem was, it would be a different woman every time, and this is what made my wife start to feel nervous. She's firmly convinced that men are influenced by the company they keep, and she felt it was really too dangerous for me to continue to interact with him, or—to be more precise—she felt it was too dangerous for *her*. She forgot that I am a decent and dutiful husband and began to issue frequent warnings, and her warnings were full of threats: she would tell me that if I behaved like Morning Tang, I would have disaster staring me in the face. She described all the details of what it would be like once disaster struck, or all the details she could think of. The trouble was, she always had a rich imagination in this area, and as a result I was growing more and more timid.

But Morning Tang is a careless, clumsy fellow, and he completely failed to pick up on the fact that my wife was so wary of him. Although I'd dropped hints lots of times, it made absolutely no impression on him. He could be quite obtuse. So it was that one day he sat down on our sofa and said loudly, "I see my friends getting married one after the other. You were first, and then Chen Lida, then Fang Hong, and then Li Shuhai. All four of you did exactly the same thing, marrying the first woman you met. I don't understand why you were all in such a hurry to get married. Why didn't you go out with a few more women first? Why not enjoy a free and independent life, like me? Why do you want to find a woman to tie you down, tie you down so tightly you can't even breathe? Now, all I need to do is just think of you guys and I can't help bursting out laughing. As soon as you open your mouths now, you're all so anxious about the reaction, especially you—you can't say two sentences without looking at your wife. Don't you get tired of that? But there's still time—you're not old yet, after all. You've still got a chance to meet other women. Shall I introduce to one sometime?"

That's Morning Tang for you. As soon as he gets going, he forgets himself. He forgot that my wife was stir-frying something in the kitchen, and given how loud his voice was, she heard every single word he said. So my wife marched out, her face livid, giving Morning Tang a prod with her wok, as the oil inside sputtered and spattered all over the place. "Get out of here," she said. "Get out of my house."

Morning Tang's face twisted with alarm. He beat a hasty retreat, his two hands groping for support on the sofa as he stumbled backward, and he didn't even have time to cast a glance my way before taking to his heels. I had never before seen such a look of sheer terror. I knew it wasn't my wife he feared as much as the hot wok she was holding. Its spattering din took the steam out of his sails that day, and it had been more than a year since he had stepped inside my door.

Now, on this hot August night, he suddenly appeared, came into my house, and had a re-encounter with my wife. By this time she was already on her feet, and when she saw Morning Tang she gave a friendly smile. "Oh, it's you. You haven't been to see us for a long time."

Morning Tang chuckled. It was obvious he remembered the hot wok. He stood there, somewhat ill at ease, until my wife pointed at the straw mat on the floor. "Come and sit down."

He glanced at the mat, but remained standing. I raised the rattling fan so that it blew in his direction, and my wife took a soda out of the refrigerator and handed it to him. He wiped the sweat off his face as he drank. "Why don't you sit down?" I said.

Now an ingratiating smile appeared on his face. "I don't dare go home," he said. "I have run into trouble."

"What kind of trouble?" I was taken aback.

He glanced at my wife. "There's a woman I've been . . . She's married, and now her husband is waiting for me outside my apartment . . ."

I realized what had happened. A jealous husband had been moved to a towering rage, and now he was bent on giving my friend Morning Tang a bloody head. My wife picked up the remote and after changing a couple of channels began to watch a program with interest. She could afford to give the matter no further thought, but I couldn't do that, for Morning Tang was my friend, after all. "What shall we do?" I said.

"Could you see me home?" he said, pathetically.

I needed to see my wife's reaction. She was sitting on the mat watching the TV, and I was hoping she would turn her head and look at me, but she didn't do that. So I had to ask her. "Can I see him home?"

My wife was still watching TV. "I don't know," she said.

"She says she doesn't know," I said to Morning Tang. "That being the case, I can't tell whether or not I can see you home."

Morning Tang shook his head. "When I was coming here," he said, "I passed Chen Lida's place, and Fang Hong's place too. And if I'd wanted to go to Li Shuhai's place, that would have been more convenient. Why did I come to you first? You know, though we haven't seen each other for a year, we are still best friends, and that's why I came to see you first. I never thought this would be your response, to say you can't tell. Why don't you just say straight out you don't want to?"

"I didn't say I didn't want to, I just said I can't tell."

"What do you mean you can't tell?"

"'Can't tell' means . . ." I glanced at my wife. "It's not that I don't want to, it's that my wife doesn't want me to. If she doesn't want me to, there's nothing I can do about it. I can go with you all right, but once I go I won't be allowed back home again—she'll lock me out and not let me in. I can stay at your house for a day, or two days, or even a month, but I'll have to go back home sooner or later, and once I do that my life will be a misery. Do you understand? It's not that I'm unwilling to go, but she just won't let me . . ."

"I didn't say that," my wife spoke up. She turned to Morning Tang. "Don't believe what he tells you. Now he's so intent on presenting himself as a pitiful creature, but the fact is he's a real tyrant at home. He insists on having the final word on everything, and it just takes the slightest thing to go wrong for him to get in one of his rages. He's smashed three glasses already this month . . ."

I interrupted her. "I really am afraid of you. Morning Tang can vouch for it."

Morning Tang nodded his head repeatedly. "That's right, he really is scared of you. We can all see that."

My wife looked at us and laughed, as we stood there awkwardly, then turned to Morning Tang with a smile. "How many people are waiting outside your apartment?"

"Just one," he said.

"Does he have a knife?"

"No."

"How do you know he doesn't? He would hide it in his pocket."

"Impossible," he said. "All he's wearing is a T-shirt and a pair of shorts. There's no way he could conceal a knife."

My wife's fears had been allayed. "Don't stay out too late," she said to me.

I nodded immediately. "I'll leave now and be back soon."

Morning Tang was clearly delighted by this unexpected development. Rather than turning around and making a prompt departure, he stood there and launched into an elaborate tribute to my wife's liberal-mindedness. "I knew you'd understand, otherwise I wouldn't have come here first. I thought it over, and it was clear to me that of all my friends' wives you are the most reasonable. Fang Hong's wife is so weird. Chen Lida's wife is a shrew. Li Shuhai's wife is always so keen on lecturing people. You're the only one who listens to reason, you're the best . . ."

Saying this, Morning Tang turned to me. "You're a lucky devil."

I thought that if he went on bullshitting like this much longer, my wife might well change her mind, so I gave him a kick. I kicked him so hard it must have hurt, for he gave a stifled "Ow!" but immediately caught on. "We're off now," he told my wife.

Just as we were going out the door, she called me back. I thought she had changed her mind, but all she did was tell me quietly, "Don't you go first. Let them go ahead of you."

I nodded reassuringly. "Got it."

After leaving my house, Morning Tang and I went first to Li Shuhai's house. Just as he had predicted, Li Shuhai's wife gave Morning Tang a long lecture. She had just taken a shower and was sitting in front of the fan combing her hair, and the water droplets shaken free by her comb blew like spittle onto Morning Tang's face, forcing him to stretch out a hand frequently to wipe away the moisture. "Didn't I warn you ages ago?" she said. "Didn't I tell you that if you carried on this way, sooner or later someone's going to break your leg? Li Shuhai, didn't I say that?"

Our friend Li Shuhai sat there, saying nothing. It embarrassed him to hear his wife scolding his friend in such a tone of voice, but he still nodded his head ever so slightly. "Morning Tang, it's not that you're a bad person," his wife went on. "In fact, your only problem is you're such a skirt-chaser. It wouldn't be a big deal if you went out with single girls, but when you start seducing other people's wives, that's really too much. The other couple has a perfectly good marriage in the first place, but once you start butting in, their happiness turns into suffering and you break up a once-contented family. If there is a child involved, it's even worse for the kid. Just think, if you were to seduce me, how miserable Li Shuhai would be! Isn't that right, Li Shuhai?"

Her use of such a personal example made her husband quite uneasy, but she was oblivious to this. "That's the way you operate," she continued. "You build your happiness on other people's suffering, but sooner or later you'll get your comeuppance. Someone's going to beat the hell out of you, and in your case even if they beat you to death nobody's going to shed any tears. Remember what I'm telling you: If you refuse to clean up your act, you're going to come to a bad end. Now, there are people waiting for you outside your apartment, isn't that right?"

Morning Tang nodded. "That's true, you've got a point. I've had bad luck recently. The women I see all turn out to be with guys who want to pick a damn fight with me."

Then Morning Tang and I, along with Li Shuhai, proceeded to Fang Hong's house. We sat down in his living room, eating popsicles that he had taken out of the refrigerator. We watched Fang Hong, shirtless, go into the bedroom, and heard the murmur of voices on the other side of the door. We knew he was telling his wife what had happened and persuading her to let him go out on this hot night to lend Morning Tang a helping hand.

The bedroom door was open just a crack. We could see that the light inside was dimmer than the living room and we could hear their voices rise and fall. They were doing their utmost to talk quietly, so it sounded as though they weren't talking so much as panting for breath.

After finishing the popsicles, we watched the head of the fan swing back and forth, blowing the hot air onto our sweating bodies. The three of us looked at one another and smiled, then stood up and took a couple of steps, then sat down again. We waited for a long time, and Fang Hong finally emerged. He carefully closed the bedroom door behind him and stood there looking grim. Then he pulled a white T-shirt down over his head and adjusted it. "Let's go," he said.

Now there were four of us. Streaming with sweat, we walked to Chen Lida's apartment block. He lives on the sixth floor, the top floor. The four of us stood on the noisy street, surrounded by people trying to escape the heat inside their own apartments, and looked upward. We saw a light was on in Chen Lida's apartment, and we called out, "Chen Lida, Chen Lida, Chen Lida."

Chen Lida appeared on the balcony and poked his head over the balustrade. "Who's there?" he called.

"It's us."

"Who?"

"Li Shuhai, Fang Hong, Morning Tang, and me," I shouted.

"Hell, is it you guys?" Chen Lida gave a delighted cry. "Come on up."

"No, we won't," we said. "You live too high up. Better if you come down."

Now we heard a woman's voice. "Come down and do what?"

We took a closer look. Chen Lida's wife was on the balcony too. She pointed at us. "What is it you want to do?"

"Morning Tang's in trouble," I called. "We friends want to help him. Have Chen Lida come down."

"What kind of trouble is Morning Tang in?" she asked.

"There's someone waiting for him outside his house," Li Shuhai said. "He wants to settle scores with him."

"Why does this person want to settle scores with him?"

"Morning Tang has something going with this man's wife," Fang Hong said.

"I've got it now," Chen Lida's wife said. "Morning Tang's been up to his old tricks again, so that man wants to kill him."

"That's right," we said.

"It's not *that* serious," Morning Tang said.

"What's the name of the woman he seduced this time?" Chen Lida's wife asked.

We turned to him. "Who's the woman this time?"

"Stop all this calling back and forth and letting so many people hear," he said. "Can't you see them all grinning? This is going to give me a terrible reputation."

"What is Morning Tang saying?" Chen Lida's wife asked.

"He told us to stop calling back and forth," I said, "otherwise he's going to end up with a bad name."

"He already has a bad name," Chen Lida's wife shouted from the balcony.

"That's true." We agreed with her, and told him so. "Actually, you already have a bad name."

"Fuck this," he swore.

"What was that he said?" Chen Lida's wife called.

"He says you're right," we answered.

So that's how Morning Tang's friends finally reached their full complement. On this August night, in a temperature of thirty-four degrees Celsius, the five of us walked along the still-steaming street toward Morning Tang's apartment. On the way we asked him who the man was. He said he didn't know him. Then we asked him who the man's wife was. He said we didn't know her. Finally we asked, How did he manage to seduce her? "What do you think?" he said. "It's just the usual routine: first you meet her, then you take her to bed."

"That simple?" we asked.

Morning Tang appeared to find our question too absurd to merit his attention. "You think there's much more to it than there really is," he said. "That's why you guys are only fit to sleep with one woman all your lives."

We stopped to buy cold drinks and stood outside the store, discussing how to handle the resentful cuckold. Li Shuhai said we should ignore him: all we had to do was see Morning Tang back to his house and let the husband know that Morning Tang has four friends like us, and the man would quickly give up on his crazy ideas. Fang Hong took the view that we should say a few words to the man, make him understand there was really no point in him giving Morning Tang a hard time, it was with his wife that he had scores to settle. What I said was: If it comes to a fight, what shall we do? Chen Lida said: If it came to a fight, all we had to do was simply stand to one side and cheer. Chen Lida felt that with us four to pep him up, Morning Tang would be sure to get the better of his adversary.

As we were debating, Morning Tang remained silent, and when we directly solicited his opinion we discovered he was busily casting flirtatious glances at a pretty girl. He hadn't heard a word we were saying. We noticed that his eyes were gleaming. A few feet away to his right, a girl with shoulder-length hair was drinking a soda. She was wearing a black tank top and a long skirt with a floral pattern. As we sized her up, she turned her head a couple of times to look at us, and Morning Tang, of course, was included in her glance, though the glance seemed casual enough. After finishing her drink, she put her Coke bottle on the counter and walked briskly away. She looked pretty stunning, the way she held herself. We watched as she stepped along the sidewalk, and then we watched in surprise as Morning Tang began to follow her. "Morning Tang!" we couldn't help but cry.

He turned and gave a chuckle, then moved off smartly, to stay close behind the pretty girl.

We were speechless. Now he was off on a search for new happiness, we realized. But what kind of time was this to choose? An enraged man was waiting outside his apartment, gnashing his teeth in his eagerness to destroy him. He had called us out from our homes, made us walk so far we were bathed in sweat, insisted we see him safely back to his house, but now he had forgotten all about that, abandoned us in front of a convenience store, and left without saying goodbye.

So we unleashed a torrent of abuse, denounced him as incorrigible, cursed him as a useless son of a bitch. We predicted he would come to a bad end. We were certain that one of these days he would be infected with syphilis, syphilis so bad his flesh would rot. At the same time we vowed never again to get involved in his affairs. Even if he ended up with his legs broken, his eyes gouged out, his balls cut off, we would just act as though nothing had happened.

We cursed till we were blue in the face, till our energy was spent, and then we quieted down. We stood there, looking at one another, and after a moment we started to wonder, What do we do now? "Do we go back home?" I asked.

None of them answered, and I realized this was a really dumb suggestion. Immediately I corrected myself. "No," I said. "We're not going to go home."

They understood straightaway what I had in mind. "Right," they said. "We're in no hurry to go home."

We realized it had been several years since we last got

together. If it hadn't been for Morning Tang, our wives wouldn't have let us out, and we suddenly became aware how rare an opportunity this was. We headed for a little bar across the street.

That night, we finally enjoyed another drinking bout, we talked endlessly, forgetting the passage of time, and none of us wanted to go home. Again and again we recalled those days when there were no women to bother us. What a wonderful time that was, when we walked forever through the streets, singing our heads off; when we muttered dirty remarks as we checked out the pretty girls; when we smashed the street lamps all along the block; when we knocked on doors in the middle of the night and ran away before the people could get out of bed and open the door; when we shut ourselves in a room with the windows closed and smoked like chimneys until the fog grew thicker and thicker, until we could hardly see one another. How many pranks did we used to play? How many times did we laugh so hard our guts ached? Some evenings we would pool together all the cash in our pockets and splurge it on beer. Later we would throw one of the empties into the air and then toss up another, making the two bottles collide in the air, shatter in the air, so the shards of glass fell to the ground like hail. We called this game Mid-Air Collisions.

ON THE BRIDGE

L et's . . ."

As he spoke, he turned his face toward her and the sunlight glittered on the black frames of his glasses. His gaze seemed to perch on top of her head like a ladder, only for him to peer off into the distance as though looking over the rim of a grassy knoll. She took her weight off the railings of the bridge, as she waited for him to say "Let's go" or "Let's go home now."

She stood there tautly, her leg bent, ready to take a step forward. But he did not finish what he was going to say.

He continued to lean against the parapet, his eyes darting back and forth like a kite that has lost its string. She relaxed her tensed posture. "What are you looking at?" she asked.

He began to cough, but it wasn't the kind of cough that you get with a cold, it was the kind of cough that you make when clearing your throat. What was he planning to say? She saw his lips part and his teeth press down on his lower lip. A throng of shouting schoolchildren poured onto the bridge, waving their satchels, and threw themselves against the parapet, as evenly spaced as a row of sparrows perched on a telephone line. A tug was approaching, its whistle blowing, a long string of barges trailing behind, and they were waiting for it to pass underneath.

A cloud of black diesel smoke had enveloped the bridge, and then the children's mouths opened and closed with a pop, and white spittle swung in an arc toward the boats below. A dozen or so barges slid one by one beneath the bridge, to be baptized by the children's saliva. The people standing at the prow of the tug waved their hands to block the spittle, as though attempting to evade arrows that were speeding toward them. Only by futile cursing could they vent their outrage. Their dog made a more impressive show of indignation, barking furiously as it ran back and forth the full length of the boat, as if racing along a street. The dog's performance captivated the children, who now forgot to carry on making a nuisance of themselves and instead watched the dog with rapt attention, at the same time filling the air with their piercing laughter.

Once again he said: "Let's . . ."

She watched him, waiting for him to continue.

It had been about a week since he had suddenly begun to be concerned about her period. This was something new. They had been married five years, and one day he was lying on the bed—it was after lunch, he was dressed and still with his shoes on—and he said he didn't plan on having a real nap. Clutching a corner of the quilt, he lay sprawled across the bed. "I'll just have a quick lie-down," he said with a yawn.

She was sitting on the sofa by the window, knitting a scarf for him. Winter was still a long way off, but better safe than sorry, as she liked to say. The autumn sunshine radiated in, tickling her neck with its warmth and casting a glow on her left hand. These sensations, and the sight of her husband peacefully reclined on the bed, gave her a contented feeling.

It was then that her truck-driver husband sat up, as abruptly as a vehicle that brakes suddenly when speeding. "Has it come?" he asked.

She was startled. "Has what come?"

Without his glasses, his eyes bulged. "Your monthly, your period, that old friend of yours," he said testily.

She laughed out loud. "Old friend" was her word for it. The two of them had known each other for well over ten years now, and this old friend of hers would come and see her every month, leaving a cramp in her belly as a calling card. She shook her head: her old friend had not yet arrived.

"Should be here by now." He put his glasses on as he spoke.

"It is time," she agreed.

"Then why the hell isn't it here?"

He appeared agitated. On such a clear and mild afternoon, in the middle of a nice nap, he had suddenly jumped up, but it wasn't because of anything big, it was just to ask her if her period had started. His attitude struck her as so comical, it made her laugh. But he seemed to have something weighing on his mind. He sat on the edge of the bed, his head tilted toward her. "Shit," he said, "are you pregnant?"

It was a mystery to her why he was reacting this way. Even if she was pregnant, this wasn't a disaster. "You've got to give me a son," he had told her when they married. "It's a son I want, not a daughter."

"Didn't you want a son?" she asked.

"No!" He practically shouted. "We can't have a child. If we have a child now, it . . . it's going to be awkward."

"What's awkward about it?" She stood up. "We're husband and wife—it's all legal . . . I didn't sneak into your bed through the back door, you know. We were married with all the proper trimmings, so what's the problem? Didn't you rent two cars and three vans for the wedding?"

"That's not what I mean." He dismissed her remarks with a wave of his hand.

"Then what *do* you mean?"

In the week that followed, he was consumed with anxiety

about her old friend. Every time he came back home after a job, she would hear the heavy thud of impatient footsteps on the stairs, along with the crisp clink of keys, and she knew very soon he would open the door and appear before her. After a glance at the balcony he would say dejectedly, "You haven't washed your underwear?"

Hearing that she had, he clutched at a sliver of hope. "Has it come?" he asked.

"No." She kept it simple.

This would take the wind out of his sails, and he would flop down on the sofa and say with a sigh: "I really don't feel like being a father right now."

She was baffled by his attitude. His paranoia about her being pregnant seemed abnormal. "What's up with you?" she said. "Why are you so afraid of me being pregnant?"

At moments like this he would look at her pathetically and not say anything. Her heart would soften; she would tell herself not to be so hard on him and try to see things his way, make him feel better. "I'm just five days late. Do you remember? Once it came ten days later than usual."

Behind his glasses a glimmer appeared in his eyes. "Is that possible?"

She saw a naive smile appear on his face. Yesterday he smiled in just that innocent way when he asked, "Are you using a panty liner?"

"I don't need it yet," she said.

"You have to," he said. "If you don't use a panty liner, it'll never come."

"That's ridiculous." She didn't take him seriously.

This provoked him. "If you're fishing and you don't use bait, how can you catch fish?" he cried.

So she put on a panty liner—with childish obstinacy he had insisted she do this. When she thought of this as fishing and how, in the eyes of her husband, her panty liner was fish bait, she couldn't help but laugh. If it weren't for his naive expression, there was no way she would have given in. Sometimes she would puzzle over the fact that in all these five years he had never shown such concern for the arrival of her old friend. After waking from his nap that day, he seemed to have become a different person. She didn't spend a lot of time thinking about the implications of this change, being more conscious that the late arrival of her period was making her nervous too. In the past, she had never paid much attention to her periods, or at most she would grouse a bit when she had cramps in her belly, but now she had to take it seriously, for she was beginning to believe she maybe *was* pregnant.

What's more, this is what he believed too, for he had lost hope that her period would take the bait.

"You're pregnant, no doubt about it." He smiled. "You're going to have to bite the bullet."

She knew what he was getting at. Letting those chilly instruments into her womb, that was what he meant. "I want this baby," she said.

"Listen." He sat back in the sofa, the personification of patience. "It's too soon to have a child, we don't have enough money. Your salary is only enough to pay for a nanny. The monthly expenses for a baby would burn up two months' pay."

"We won't have a nanny," she said.

"This is going to be the death of me." He was getting hot under the collar.

"I won't make you do the work. I'll look after the baby."

"You're still a kid yourself. To have one kid is as much as I can manage. If there are two of you," he said mournfully, "how am I going to survive?"

After a moment, he got to his feet and waved his hand in the air to indicate that the decision had been made. "Get rid of it," he said.

"You're not the one who has to do that," she replied. "And if I have the baby you won't have to share the pain either."

"You're just twenty-four, and I'm just one year older, think about it . . ."

Now, the two of them were heading toward the hospital. It was afternoon, and they were on their way to confirm she was pregnant. The street was quiet, and he lowered his voice as he walked. "Think about it, if we have a kid now, we'll have a grandchild before we're fifty. You'll be a grandma at forty, when you've still got your looks and figure and whatnot. When you're walking in the street, people will think you're in your thirties, but you'll be a grandma. What a pain!"

"I've got no problem with being a grandmother." She threw him a glance.

"But I have a problem with being a grandfather!" he bellowed. Then he noticed people were looking at him. "Damn it," he fumed, "these past few days you haven't listened to a word I've said."

She smiled thinly, but seeing his livid expression said simply, "Then just keep quiet."

As they walked toward the hospital, he rattled on. It was a last-ditch struggle, his effort to crack open a stone with drops of rain. She began to feel uneasy: with her husband already so fearful of their child's arrival, what would it be like when she actually gave birth? It was this thought that triggered her uneasiness. She stood still, and became aware of a cramp in her belly. It was as though she heard the sound of something moving, and a warm current slowly began to flow downward. She knew what this meant and breathed a sigh of relief: she would no longer feel uneasy and her husband would no longer quiver with rage. "Forget about the hospital," she said.

He was still intent on persuading her, and hearing her say this he brusquely waved his hand, thinking she was angry. "All right," he said, "I'll stop."

"My old friend has arrived."

Having said this, she smiled, while he looked at her in disbelief. Then she walked off toward the public toilets on her right, and he waited for her by the steps of the theater. When she came out with a smile and a nod, he knew for sure that her old friend had appeared. He gave a chuckle, and he was in a fine mood all afternoon, turning somber only when they walked onto the bridge. It was then that he looked grave and lost in thought.

She stood by his side, watching the long line of barges receding into the distance, as the children moved away in a clamor of voices. It was quite some time since he last spoke. When he had said, "Let's . . . ," she thought he wanted to go home, but he never made a move. She smiled sweetly, for she could imagine what he planned to say. "Let's not have dinner at home," he would say. "We'll go out to a restaurant." He would have a complacent smile on his face. "We should celebrate," he'd say, "and have a really good time." He would lick his lower lip. "I'm going to have a pint of draft beer," he'd say. He could always find an excuse to party: even when there was no particular reason, he would tell her, "I'm in a good mood today, let's celebrate."

Now his glance, so evasive earlier, rested on her face, and he drew a deep breath. "Let's . . ."

He paused, then carried on, his voice hoarse. "Let's get a divorce."

She looked at him blankly, as though she hadn't understood what he had just said, and he wheeled away from her, saying with an awkward smile, "See you later."

Her mouth slightly ajar, she watched as he put his hands in his pockets and walked away as if he hadn't a care in the world. The breeze lifted his hair. His movements were so quick, even before she had time to respond he had already merged smoothly with the flow of people who had just got off work, concealing his own confusion. As he was leaving her, his whole body contracted, and when he took that step forward his legs felt as stiff as two bamboo poles, as though it had become impossible to bend at the knees. But in her eyes he was walking away as if nothing had happened.

The rapidity of his flight made her realize that what he said was not a joke, and she felt her breath come with a flapping sound, like wind blowing on a wall where a piece of paper has been posted.

SWELTERING SUMMER

Having a boyfriend offers many conveniences—for instance, when you want to see a movie, there'll be someone to buy your ticket and supply you with prunes and olives—so many it will take you days to finish them. If it's a question of going off sightseeing, then boyfriends come in even more handy, paying for food and accommodation, carrying this or that for you . . . Sponsors, that's the word for them."

As Wen Hong spoke, she scanned the faces within view.

It was a summer evening, and after her shower Li Ping was lying in her nightgown on a rattan couch that lay in the street outside her home. The street, which was not very wide in the first place, had become so crowded with people trying to cool off that it was now as narrow as a corridor. Bamboo beds, rattan chairs, and other furniture that really belonged indoors had been moved outside, and even mosquito nets were unfurled. The locals generated a constant buzz of noise, like a flock of bees attracted by rapeseed blossom, and the street was as packed tight as a strip of fresh green growth. As Li Ping lay on her couch, her long hair cascaded over the back of her pillow, where it was blown about by an electric fan she had laid on the ground. Wen Hong, sitting next to her, spoke up once more. "Hey, I see a sponsor now."

"Who?" Li Ping put her hands behind her head and gave her hair a shake.

"Li Qigang," Wen Hong said. "Shall I call him over?"

Li Ping gave a sudden giggle. "That moron?"

"He's seen us," Wen Hong said.

"He's coming over?"

Wen Hong nodded. "Yes."

"That geek tried to go out with me," Li Ping said.

"He asked me out, too," Wen Hong whispered.

Both girls burst out laughing. Li Qigang walked up to them with a smile on his face. "What's so funny?" he asked.

The girls laughed all the more loudly, one almost bent over double, the other clasping her knees as she sprawled on the couch. Li Qigang stood unflappably at their side, maintaining his smile. He was wearing a short-sleeved shirt, trousers, and shiny leather shoes. With the back of his hand he wiped away the sweat on his forehead. "Everybody's looking at you," he said.

Hearing this, the two girls stopped laughing and took a quick look around. They noticed a few people casting glances in their direction. Wen Hong straightened herself and gave her hair a good shake as Li Ping sat up and pulled her nightgown over her knees.

"You girls should get a haircut," Li Qigang said.

The two girls looked at him and then at each other.

"Do it in a page-boy style," Li Qigang went on.

Wen Hong spoke up at this point. "I like my hairstyle," she said, running her hand through her hair.

"I like your hairstyle too," Li Ping chimed in.

Wen Hong glanced at her. "Where did you have your hair done?"

"At Rougerie, the place on Zhongshan Boulevard."

"They did a really good job. That cut is all the rage in Europe these days."

Li Ping nodded. "I saw this style in a foreign magazine. It was all in English, not a single Chinese character. Your hairstyle was featured too. At the time I was really keen on doing my hair like you. Your hair really complements your face."

"Lin Jing and the other girls said the same thing." Wen Hong toyed with her hair.

Li Qigang noticed how the two girls were talking to each other and not paying him the slightest attention, so he tried to get a word in edgeways. "I still think the page-boy look is prettier. It's so cute, and besides, the weather is so hot. With long hair—"

Wen Hong interrupted him. "Aren't you hot in your long pants?"she asked.

Li Qigang looked down at his trousers. "They're wool. They don't feel hot."

Wen Hong practically screamed. "You're wearing woolen pants?"

Li Qigang nodded. "Ninety percent wool."

Wen Hong stole a glance at Li Ping. "Wow, ninety percent wool."

The two girls snickered, and Li Qigang watched them with a smile. Li Ping sat up on her rattan couch. "Why didn't you buy one hundred percent pure wool pants?" she asked.

Li Qigang squatted down and untied his laces, then took his left foot out of his shoe and placed it on Li Ping's couch. Pointing at the straight crease on his trouser leg, he said: "See this line? If it was one hundred percent wool, it wouldn't be so straight."

"You could iron it," said Li Ping.

Li Qigang nodded. "That's true, but after wearing the pants

for ten minutes, the line would disappear. Pants that are one hundred percent wool are no good."

Wen Hong reached out a hand and felt Li Qigang's trousers. "Pants this heavy will feel hot even if they're ninety percent wool," she remarked. Turning to Li Ping, she said, "What do you think?"

"You can see right away those are thick pants," Li Ping answered. "Just now, as you were coming over here, I thought you were wearing cotton pants."

Wen Hong tittered. "I thought they were serge."

With a smile, Li Qigang removed his foot from Li Ping's chair, slipped it into his shoe, and bent down to tie his shoelace. "Of course, compared to them . . ." He pointed at several youths passing by in Western-style shorts: "Compared to them, these are warmer. Long trousers are always warmer than shorts. Some people wear shorts the whole summer long and expose their chests as well, slouching around in sandals. That's okay for them, but it won't do for us. We in official positions need to maintain our image. We might get away with not wearing stylish clothes, but at least we have to look neat, don't we?"

At this point, Li Qigang took a handkerchief out of his pocket and wiped his forehead. Wen Hong and Li Ping exchanged glances and smiled conspiratorially. "Where have you people in the Cultural Bureau moved to?" Wen Hong asked.

"Tianning Monastery."

"You've moved to a temple?" cried Wen Hong.

Li Qigang nodded. "It's wonderfully cool in the summer there."

"What about the winter?" asked Li Ping.

"In the winter . . . ," Li Qigang conceded, "it's cold."

"Why don't you people in the Cultural Bureau get your-selves an office building? Look how impressive the headquarters of the Finance and Business bureaus are," Wen Hong said.

"We don't have the money," said Li Qigang. "No department has a smaller budget than we do."

"So, of people in official positions, you're the poorest."

"I wouldn't say that." Li Qigang smiled.

Li Ping looked at Wen Hong. "No matter how poor they are, they're still officials, and officials are always going to have higher status than us." She turned to Li Qigang. "Isn't that right?"

He smiled modestly. "I wouldn't say we have higher status than you, but compared to the average worker, having a job in a government agency is a bit more dignified."

The two girls chortled. Li Qigang again broached the topic of their hairstyle, repeating his recommendation. "You should really think about short hair."

Again they laughed—and all the more loudly—but he took this in stride. "Do it the way Scarlet does her hair," he went on.

"Who?" asked Wen Hong.

"Scarlet, the singer," replied Li Qigang.

"Oh," the girls responded. "I can't see what's so great about Scarlet's hairstyle," said Li Ping.

"Her face is too pointy," said Wen Hong.

Li Qigang smiled. "Next month I'm going to Shanghai to escort her here."

Hearing this the girls were taken aback, and it was a moment before Wen Hong asked, "Scarlet's coming?"

"That's right." Li Qigang gave a restrained nod.

"To give a performance?" asked Li Ping.

Li Qigang nodded. "The most expensive seats will cost fifty yuan, and even the cheapest ones will be thirty."

The girls' eyes gleamed. "You've got to get us a couple of tickets," they said.

"No problem," said Li Qigang. "I'm involved in setting up the whole event, so there's no problem at all in getting you two tickets."

"Make it complimentary tickets," said Li Ping.

"That's right," said Wen Hong, "I bet you can get your hands on lots of tickets. Give us two for free."

Li Qigang hesitated a moment. "Okay, they're on me."

The two girls beamed. "Give us the fifty-yuan seats," Li Ping said.

"We don't want the thirty-yuan ones," said Wen Hong.

"That's right," said Li Ping. "Don't make us sit in the back row, where we won't be able to see Scarlet's face."

Li Qigang again hesitated. He wiped his forehead. "I'll make every effort to get you fifty-yuan seats."

"Don't say 'make every effort,'" said Wen Hong. "It's a real letdown when someone of your position says 'make every effort.'"

Li Ping smiled. "That's exactly right. It must be a piece of cake for someone of your status to come up with a couple of superior seats."

"All right then," Li Qigang said, after a moment's reflection, "I'll get you two fifty-yuan tickets."

The two girls gave whoops of delight. Li Qigang smiled, looked at his watch, and announced that he had to attend to some business. The girls got up to see him off and, as soon as he had walked away, they murmured in almost the same breath, "What a dummy."

They giggled. "He's a real blockhead," Wen Hong said.

"Sometimes even dummies have their uses," Li Ping remarked.

The two girls giggled once again. "When was it he asked you out?" Wen Hong quietly asked.

"Last year. What about you?"

"Last year, too." They had another giggle. "How did he go about it?" Wen Hong inquired.

"He called me up," Li Ping said. "He called and asked me to meet him at the entrance to the Cultural Bureau. He said there was going to be an event. An instructor in ballroom dancing was coming from Shanghai and would teach us how to dance. So I went . . ."

"You never saw the ballroom dancing instructor."

"How did you know?"

"He made just the same kind of date with me."

"And then he asked you to go out for a stroll?"

"That's right," said Wen Hong. "Did you go for a walk with him?"

"We walked a little way, and I asked him if it was time to go for the dance lesson. He said no, what he wanted to do was go out for a walk together. I asked him what he had in mind."

"Did he say it was so you could get to know each other better?"

Li Ping nodded. "He said the same thing to you?"

"That's right," Wen Hong replied. "I asked him why he wanted us to get to know each other better."

"I asked him the same question."

"He said he wanted us to be friends, and I asked him why."

Li Ping picked this up: "He was slow to answer."

"Right," Wen Hong said. "He rubbed his chin for ages and finally said . . ."

Li Ping imitated Li Qigang's tone of voice: "To see if we fall in love."

The two girls roared with laughter. They laughed so much they couldn't stand up straight, and it was a full five minutes before they recovered. Then Li Ping said: "When I heard him say 'fall in love,' my hair stood on end."

"I was as petrified as a mouse in a cat's jaws," said Wen Hong.

Again they burst out laughing. "How did you respond?" Wen Hong asked.

"I said I wanted to go home."

"That was very civil of you," Wen Hong said. "I told him: You've got as much chance as the toad that fancied the swan."

ONE EVENING SEVERAL WEEKS LATER, Wen Hong arrived at Li Ping's apartment. Li Ping was doing herself up in front of the mirror. She had just finished combing her hair and had begun to paint her eyebrows. She had an eyebrow pencil in her hand as she opened the door, and seeing this Wen Hong asked: "Are you going out?"

Li Ping nodded and returned to her seat in front of the mirror. "I'm going to a movie."

"Who with?" Wen Hong pricked up her ears.

Li Ping smiled, but did not answer.

"You've got a boyfriend!" Wen Hong exclaimed. "Who is he?"

"You'll find out soon enough."

"So that's the way you want it." Wen Hong gave Li Ping a jab. "You have a boyfriend, and you don't even tell me."

"I'm telling you now, aren't I?"

"Then I'll stay and meet him." Wen Hong sat down on the sofa and watched Li Ping putting on her makeup. As Li Ping painted her lips, she said, "This imported lipstick is really good."

Wen Hong thought of something. "I ran into Li Qigang this morning. He was wearing an imported tie. It looked really nice."

"That singer Scarlet gave it to him," Li Ping said.

"That's right, that's what he told me," Wen Hong said. Then, with a trace of suspicion, she said, "How did you know?"

Li Ping massaged her face with both hands. "He told me."

Wen Hong smiled. "Do you know something? Scarlet likes Li Qigang."

Seeing Li Ping nodding in the mirror, Wen Hong asked: "Did you know that too?"

"Yeah," Li Ping answered.

"Did he tell you himself?"

"That's right."

"This Li Qigang . . ." Wen Hong seemed displeased. "He told me not to tell anyone, but the guy goes around himself telling lots of people."

"He hasn't told a lot of people. Just you and me, right?"

"Who knows?" said Wen Hong.

Li Ping stood up, and tried on the dress she had laid out on the bed. "How do I look?" she asked.

"You look great," said Wen Hong. "How much did he tell you?"

"About what?"

"About Scarlet chasing him."

"Not much."

Wen Hong watched as Li Ping swiveled from side to side in the mirror. "Did you know that he and Scarlet spent the night in her hotel room?"

Li Ping spun around and stared at Wen Hong. "He told you that too!"

"That's right." Wen Hong was rather pleased. Then she noticed something. "He told you too?"

Li Ping could see there was something odd about Wen Hong's expression. She turned around and said offhandedly, "I asked him about it."

Wen Hong smiled. "I didn't ask him. It was he who told me."

A fleeting smile appeared on Li Ping's face. Wen Hong laid her arms on the back of the sofa and gazed at her friend's figure. "This Li Qigang is actually quite classy, don't you think?"

"That's right," said Li Ping. "Otherwise, why would a woman as pretty and popular as Scarlet take a fancy to him?"

Wen Hong nodded. She put her hands in her lap. "Actually Scarlet is no beauty. From a distance she looks good, but when you get close up she's not so pretty."

"When did you get to look at her close up?"

"I haven't," Wen Hong said. "It was Li Qigang who told me that."

Li Ping looked unhappy. "What did he say exactly?"

Wen Hong seemed pleased. "He said Scarlet isn't as pretty as me."

"Not as pretty as you?"

"Not as pretty as us."

"Us?"

"You and me."

"He mentioned my name?"

"Yes."

"That's not what you said in the beginning."

Wen Hong looked at Li Ping in surprise. "Is something wrong?"

"Not at all." Li Ping gave a quick laugh, then turned around and looked at herself in the mirror. She wiped the corner of her eye with her left hand.

"If the two of them spent the night in a hotel," Wen Hong said, "what do you think they did?"

"I don't know," Li Ping said. "He didn't tell you?"

"No, he didn't," Wen Hong said, inquiringly.

"Probably nothing happened," Li Ping said.

"No," Wen Hong said. "They put their arms around each other."

"It was Scarlet who put her arms around him," Li Ping blurted out.

The girls looked at each other, stunned. Li Ping was the first to laugh, and then Wen Hong. Just as Li Ping sat down, there was a knock at the door, and as she was about to get up again, Wen Hong said, "I'll get it for you."

She walked over and opened the door, to find a neatly dressed Li Qigang standing smiling on the doorstep. He gave a start, clearly not expecting to be greeted by Wen Hong. After a moment he tilted his head round the door and said to Li Ping, as she walked toward him, "You look terrific."

Wen Hong heard a chortle from her friend, who walked past her and out the door, then reached back to grasp the doorknob. Wen Hong suddenly realized what was what, and hurried out as Li Ping closed the door behind her.

On the sidewalk, Li Ping took Li Qigang's arm. "Do you have a ticket?" he asked Wen Hong.

She shook her head. "No."

Li Ping, her hand on Li Qigang's arm, turned away. After a couple of steps, she looked over her shoulder. "Wen Hong, we've got to go. Drop by some time."

Wen Hong, nodding, watched them stroll off. When they had gone twenty yards or so, she headed off in the other direction, giving a "Humph!" as she went.

TIMID AS A MOUSE

1

There's an expression that fits me to a T: timid as a mouse. That's what my teacher said, back when I was in primary school. This was one autumn, I remember, in Chinese class. The teacher stood on the dais; he was wearing a dark blue cotton jacket over a clean white shirt. I was sitting in the middle of the front row, looking up at him. He held a textbook in his hand and his fingers were coated with red, white, and yellow chalk dust. As he read the lesson aloud, his face and his hands and his book towered above me and his spittle was constantly spraying my face, so that I had repeatedly to raise my hand and wipe it off. He noticed that his spittle was sprinkling my face and that I would blink my eyes fearfully when it came flying my way, so he stopped reciting and put down his book, then stepped down from the dais and walked over to me, stretched out his chalk-stained hand and patted my face, as though giving it a wash. Then he went back to the desk to retrieve his book and began to walk around the classroom as he recited the lesson. He had wiped dry the spittle on my face, but in so doing had left my face blotched with red, white, and yellow chalk dust. My classmates began to titter, because my face now looked as gaudy as a butterfly.

It was at this point that the teacher came to the place in the text where the expression "timid as a mouse" was introduced. He laid the upturned book against his thigh. "What is meant by 'timid as a mouse'?" he said. "It's an expression, used to describe somebody who has no more courage than a mouse . . ."

His mouth stayed open, for he had something more he wanted to say. "For example . . ."

His eyes scanned the room. He wanted to find an analogy. The teacher loved analogies. If he was trying to explain the word "irrepressible," he would have Lü Qianjin stand up and he'd say, "For example, Lü Qianjin—he's irrepressible. It's as though he's got a straw stuck up his ass all the time—he'll just never sit still." Or when he came to the expression "if the lips are gone, the teeth are cold," he would ask Zhao Qing to stand up: "For example, Zhao Qing. Why does he look so miserable? That's because his father died. His father is the lips, and if the lips are gone the teeth will chatter." That's the way our teacher made his analogies: "For example, Song Hai . . . For example, Fang Dawei . . . For example, Lin Lili . . . For example, Hu Qiang . . . For example, Liu Jisheng . . . For example, Xu Hao . . . For example, Sun Hongmei . . ."

Now he spotted me. "Yang Gao," he said.

I got to my feet. The teacher looked at me a moment, then waved his hand. "Sit down."

I sat down. The teacher tapped his fingers on the desk. "All those afraid of tigers, raise your hands."

Everybody in the class raised their hands. The teacher surveyed the room. "Put your hands down."

We put our hands down. "All those afraid of dogs, raise your hands," the teacher said.

When I raised my hand, I heard a lot of giggles. I found that the girls had raised their hands, but none of the other boys had. "Put your hands down," the teacher said.

The girls and I put our hands down. "All those afraid of geese, raise your hands," the teacher now said.

Once more I raised my hand. The whole classroom erupted in laughter. This time I was the only person to raise a hand—none of the girls had. My classmates were in hysterics. The teacher did not laugh; he had to tap sharply on the desk to restore order. He looked out into the room, not at me. "Put your hand down," he said.

I was the only person who had to do that. Then he directed his gaze at me. "Yang Gao."

I stood up. He pointed at me. "For example, Yang Gao, he's even afraid of geese . . ."

He paused for a moment, then went on, in a loud voice, "'Timid as a mouse'—that's Yang Gao."

2

It's true I'm timid as a mouse. I don't dare go near the river and I don't dare climb trees, and that's because, before my father died, he would often say: "Yang Gao, you can go play in the school playground or along the sidewalk or at a classmate's house. Any place is fine—just don't go near the river and don't go climbing trees. If you fall into the river, you might drown. If you fall out of a tree, you might break your neck."

That's why I was standing there in the summer sun, watching from a distance, as Lü Qianjin, Zhao Qing, Song Hai, and Fang Dawei, along with Hu Qiang, Liu Jisheng, and Xu Hao, played about in the river, watching as they splashed water, watching their glossy black heads and shiny white behinds.

One after another they dived into the water and stuck their behinds into the air. They called this game "Selling Pumpkins." "Yang Gao, come on in!" they shouted. "Yang Gao, hurry up and sell a pumpkin!"

I shook my head. "I would drown!" I said.

"Yang Gao, do you see Lin Lili and Sun Hongmei?" they asked. "See—they're in the water. Girls get in the water, see? You're a boy—how come you won't join us?"

Sure enough, I could see Lin Lili and Sun Hongmei wading about in the river in their bright underpants and cheerful tank tops, but still I shook my head and repeated, "I would drown!"

Knowing I wouldn't go in the river, they told me to climb a tree instead. "Yang Gao," they said, "if you won't come in, then go climb a tree."

"I can't climb trees," I said.

"All of *us* can," they said. "How come you're the only one who can't?"

"If I fall, I might break my neck," I told them.

They stood in a line in the water and Lü Qianjin said, "One, two, three, shout . . ."

They shouted out in unison, "There's a phrase 'timid as a mouse,' and who is it about?"

"Me," I murmured.

"We didn't hear that," Lü Qianjin shouted.

So I said again, "It refers to me."

After hearing this, they no longer stood in a line but went back into the water, and the water again began to roil and seethe. I sat down in front of a tree and went on watching as they fooled around in the river and sold those white pumpkins of theirs.

I am a biddable boy. That's not my word—that's what my mother says. She often sings her son's praises to other people: "Our Yang Gao is just the most biddable boy. He's so obedient, and such a hard worker. He'll do whatever you tell him to do. He's never got in trouble outside the house and never got into fights with people. Why, I've never heard him say any dirty words . . ."

My mother's right. I never curse people and never pick a fight with anybody. But there are always people who like to come over and curse me or pick a fight. They roll their sleeves up above their elbows and their pants up above their knees, block my path, and poke me on the nose, spit in my face and say, "Yang Gao, have you got the guts to fight with us?"

"No, I don't," I tell them.

"In that case," they say, "do you have the guts to curse us?"

"No, I don't have the guts for that either," I tell them.

"In that case," they say, "we're going to curse *you*. Listen up! You cretin! Cretin! Cretin! Cretin, and asshole too!"

Even girls—girls like Lin Lili and Sun Hongmei—give me a hard time. Once I heard other girls say to them, "You only know how to bully us girls. If you're so tough, why don't you go pick a fight with a boy?"

"Who said we're afraid of boys?" they replied.

They came over and stood on either side of me, sandwiching me between them. "Yang Gao," they said, "we want to pick a fight with a boy, so how about if we pick a fight with you? We won't both fight with you, we'll fight one to one. So pick between us, Lin Lili or Sun Hongmei."

I shook my head. "No, I'm not going to pick between you. I'm not going to fight with you."

I wanted to get away, but Lin Lili stretched out an arm and held me back. "You don't want to fight with us?" she said. "Or you don't have the guts to fight with us?"

"I don't have the guts to fight with you," I said.

Lin Lili let me go, but then Sun Hongmei grabbed me. "We can't let him off that easy," she said. "We need to have him say 'timid as a mouse.'"

So Lin Lili put it to me, "There's a phrase 'timid as a mouse.' Who does it refer to?"

"It refers to me," I said.

3

When my father was alive, he would say to my mother, "This boy Yang Gao is too much of a sissy. Even when he was six, he didn't dare talk to people. When he was eight, he was too scared to sleep by himself. Even when he was ten, he couldn't summon up the courage to lean against the parapet on the bridge. Now he's twelve, and geese still scare him."

My dad was right. When I ran into a flock of geese, my legs would turn to jelly and there was nothing I could do about it. What frightened me the most was when they charged toward me, stretching out their necks and flapping their wings. I was forced to keep going in the other direction, past Lü Qianjin's house. Past Song Hai's house I went, and Fang Dawei's and Lin Lili's, but those geese just kept on chasing me, honk honk honk, in full cry all the way. Once they pursued me right out of Yang Family Lane and kept on my tail the full length of

Liberation Road, right up to the school. As they followed me across the playground, still honking away, people gathered to watch and I heard Lü Qianjin shout, "Yang Gao, give them a kick!"

So I swiveled around, took aim at a goose in the middle of the pack, and gave it a little kick. But that just made them honk more fiercely and lunge toward me more aggressively. I turned right round and kept on going.

"Kick them!" Lü Qianjin and the others were shouting. "Yang Gao, kick them!"

I kept on moving as fast as I could, and as I went I shook my head. "They're not afraid of my kicks."

"Throw stones at them!" Lü Qianjin and the others shouted.

"I don't have any stones," I said.

They laughed uproariously. "Then you'd better run for your life!" they shouted.

I shook my head again. "I can't run. As soon as I do, you'll laugh at me."

"We're laughing at you already!" they said.

I took a good look at them. They were laughing so hard their mouths were open and their eyes were closed and their bodies were bent double. I thought to myself, it's true, they *are* laughing at me, so I began to run.

"Geese's eyes are the problem," my mother explained to me later. "Geese see everything as smaller than it really is, and that's why they're so bold.

"Seen through a goose's eye," she went on, "our front door is like a hollow in the wall, our window is like the opening in the crotch of your pants, our house is as small as a hen's nest . . ."

What about me, then? That evening, when I lay in bed, I

kept wondering how big I was in the eyes of a goose. I decided the biggest I could possibly be was only as big as another goose.

4

When I was little, I often heard them talking about how timid I was. By "them" I mean Lü Qianjin's mother and Song Hai's mother, also Lin Lili's mother and Fang Dawei's mother. In the summer they would sit in the shade under the trees and gossip about other people's affairs. They would chatter away, even louder than the cicadas in the tree above, they'd yak and yak until the conversation came round to me. They would talk about how often I'd been a coward, and once they talked about my father too and said he was just as much of a coward as I was.

I was upset when I heard that, and went and sat down by myself on the doorsill. I'd just heard something I didn't know before. They said my father was the slowest driver in the world. They said nobody wanted to ride in his truck, because a trip that would take other drivers three hours my father wouldn't manage to complete in five. Why? They said it was because my father was too timid. They said he got scared if he drove at all fast. Scared of what? Scared he'd crash and die.

Lü Qianjin and the others saw me sitting alone on the doorsill. They came over, stood in front of me, and said with a laugh: "Your father *is* a coward, just like you. Your cowardice is genetic. You got it from your dad, and he got it from your granddad, and your granddad got it from your granddad's granddad . . ."

They went through a whole dozen or so of my ancestors' granddads and then asked, "Does your father have the guts to drive with his eyes closed?"

I shook my head. "I don't know," I said. "I've never asked him."

Lü Qianjin said his father could swallow a whole Yorkshire pig in one go. Lü Qianjin's father slaughtered pigs. "You've got eyes in your head," Lü Qianjin said. "You can see for yourself my father is even stouter than a Yorkshire pig."

Song Hai's father was a surgeon. Song Hai said his father regularly operated on himself. "I often wake up in the middle of the night and see my father sitting by the dining table, his head down, a flashlight gripped between his teeth so that the light shines on his belly. He's stitching himself up."

Then there's Fang Dawei's father. Fang Dawei says his father can knock a hole through a wall with just one punch. Even Liu Jisheng's father—who's so thin there's no flesh on his bones, who spends half the year in a hospital bed—Liu Jisheng says he can snap nails in half with his teeth.

"So how about your dad?" they ask. "What is it he can do? Does he have the guts to drive with his eyes closed?"

I shook my head again. "I don't know."

"Then hurry up and ask him."

After they left, I went on sitting on the doorsill, waiting for my father to return. In the late afternoon, my mother came home and saw me sitting there in a daze. "Yang Gao, what are you doing?" she asked.

"I'm sitting on the doorsill," I said.

"I can see that," she said. "What I want to know is, what are you doing sitting there?"

"I'm waiting for Father to come home," I said.

Mother started to prepare dinner. As she ladled water out of the vat to sieve the rice, she said, "Come inside and help me wash the vegetables."

I didn't go in. I stayed sitting on the doorsill, and though my mother called me time and again, I went on sitting there, right until nightfall, when my father came home. His heavy footsteps sounded slowly on the darkened street, and then he appeared at the corner, carrying that shabby old bag of his. As his black shadow approached, the light from the house shone on his foot, then climbed his legs. When it reached his chest, he stopped and bent down. His head was still in shadow as he asked, "Yang Gao, what are you doing here?"

"I was waiting for you to come home," I said. I stood up and followed him inside. He sat down in a chair and put his arms on the table. He looked at me, and that was when I asked, "Do you dare to drive with your eyes closed?"

My father smiled and shook his head. "You can't drive with your eyes closed."

"Why not?" I said. "Why can't you drive with your eyes closed?"

"If I was to drive with my eyes closed," my father said, "I'd crash and die."

5

My mother is right—I'm biddable. I've got a fine job now, on the janitorial staff at the machine plant. I am in the same factory and the same shop as Lü Qianjin. He's a fitter, so he's got oil all over his hands and all over his clothes, but he's perfectly happy. He says he's got a skilled job and he looks down on the work I do, saying my job is unskilled. It's true there's no skill involved in my job—all I have to do is take a broom and sweep the shop's concrete floor. So I don't have any skill, but I also don't have any oil on my hands or clothes, while Lü Qianjin's fingernails are dirty black. His nails have been like that ever since he came to the factory.

Actually, when we just started, it was Lü Qianjin who was the janitor and me who was the fitter. Lü Qianjin refused to be janitor and went off to see the manager, a chisel in his hand. He stuck the chisel in the manager's desk and said he would not be janitor, he insisted on being reassigned. So that's how Lü Qianjin and I came to exchange positions, with him becoming a fitter and me becoming janitor. After he became a fitter, he handed me the chisel and told me to stick it in the manager's desk just as he had. I asked him why.

"If you stick it in his desk," he said, "you won't have to be janitor anymore."

"What's wrong with being janitor?" I asked.

"Damn it, you're such a blockhead," he said. "Being janitor is the most demeaning job of all—don't you realize that yet?"

"Yes, I realize that. I know none of you are willing to be janitor."

He put his hands on my shoulders and started pushing me. "If you're clear on that, that's fine then," he said. "Off you go."

He pushed me out of the shop. I took a few steps forward, and then I turned around and went back in. Lü Qianjin blocked my path. "What are you doing back here?" he asked.

"If I stick the chisel in the manager's desk, but he still wants me to be janitor," I said, "what do I do then?"

"That's not what's going to happen!" said Lü Qianjin. "All

you need to do is stick the chisel in the desk and the manager will be scared. If he's scared, he will let you go back to being a fitter again."

I shook my head. "The manager won't get scared so easily."

"What do you mean?" said Lü Qianjin. He started pushing me again. "I scared him, didn't I?"

"You scared him," I said, "but *I* wouldn't scare him."

Lü Qianjin looked at me intently for a moment and then withdrew his hands. "You're right," he said. "You wouldn't scare the manager. You wouldn't fucking scare anybody. You were fucking born to sweep the floor."

Lü Qianjin is right. I *was* born to sweep floors. I like sweeping floors. I like sweeping the shop floor until it's squeaky clean. I like walking back and forth in the shop with the broom in my hand, and even when I sit down to take a break I like to hold the broom. The guys in the shop say, "Yang Gao, the way you hug that broom of yours, it's like you're feeling a woman up."

I know they are having a joke at my expense, but I pay them no mind, because they are always making fun. I have no idea why they love to laugh at me so much. If I'm sweeping the floor, they watch me and roar with laughter; if I'm walking along, they point at me and laugh fit to burst. When I clock in before them, they think this a great joke, and when I finish work later than them, they think that a great joke too. Actually, I start and finish just at the proper time, at the time fixed by the factory, but they make fun of me all the same, because they always start late and knock off early. "Yang Gao," Lü Qianjin once said, "everybody else starts late and finishes early, so why do you start on time and finish on time?"

"That's because I'm biddable," I told him.

He looked at me and shook his head. "No, it's because you're timid."

I feel it isn't that I am timid, it's because I like this job of mine. Lü Qianjin doesn't like his job, doesn't like this skilled fitter's job that he got with the chisel, so he comes to work late every day. Not only does he turn up late, but he often drags an old mat over to a corner of the workshop and takes a nap there. Sometimes Song Hai and Fang Dawei come over to socialize, slipping away from their posts during work hours, and when they see Lü Qianjin snoring away on that old mat of his, they shout at him to wake up. "Damn, you really know how to make yourself comfortable, don't you? Here you are, sleeping on the job. You might as well fetch your bed from home and move it right in."

At moments like these, Lü Qianjin rubs his eyes and chuckles. "You guys not working today?" he'll say.

"We're working all right," Fang Dawei and company say, "but we slipped out for a breather."

"Well, aren't you doing the same thing as me?" Lü Qianjin says. "You guys are pretty damn comfortable yourselves."

Then Fang Dawei and the others call me over. "Yang Gao, every time we come over here we see you sweeping the floor. Why don't you take a leaf out of Lü Qianjin's book and take a nap on that old mat?"

I shake my head. "I never take a nap."

"Why not?" they ask.

"I like my work," I reply, broom in hand.

Hearing this, they roared with laughter. They find this very strange. "Can you believe it?" they say. "There's still someone in the world who likes sweeping floors."

It's not strange to me, because I really do like sweeping the workshop till it's spick-and-span. I wipe all the machinery in the shop until it is squeaky clean too. Because of me, our workshop has become the cleanest in the whole plant. The people in the other shops wish they could have me working for them, but the people in our workshop won't let me go. Everybody knows that—in the plant, and outside too. Even my old classmates Lin Lili and Sun Hongmei know, because once they said, "Yang Gao, you're the best worker in your factory, but every time they award raises or assign housing, you're always left out . . . Look at that Lü Qianjin—he's always napping on the job, but he gets a raise, he gets an apartment. He does no work, but he has his finger in every pie."

"I'm not in his league," I said to them. "Lü Qianjin has ways of getting things done. But not me. I have no way of getting anything done."

"What are Lü Qianjin's ways of getting things done? What else is there to it but threatening the factory manager with a knife?"

They got that wrong. Lü Qianjin never used a knife to threaten the manager. He did use a chisel when he first got his job assignment, but later he didn't even use that. When he heard some workers were going to get raises, he went off empty-handed, went off to the manager's office every morning as though that was his workplace, not our workshop. He would go into the manager's office, sit down in one of the manager's chairs, drinking the manager's tea and smoking the manager's cigarettes, talking to the manager for hours on end. That carried on until one day the manager said to him, "Lü Qianjin, the list of those getting raises has now been approved, and your name is on it."

Lü Qianjin then returned to our workshop to work. Ever since, the old mat in the corner of the shop has never gone unoccupied—you can see a body stretched out there at all hours of the day.

Lü Qianjin's wages keep on rising, while mine never change. Lü Qianjin has tried to educate me. "Yang Gao," he said, "just think—when we first came to the plant, we had exactly the same pay. Years have passed, and I keep on napping every day and you keep on slaving away, and yet I'm paid more than you are. Do you know why that is?"

"Why?" I said.

"It's because misery is the lot of the timid, and fortune favors the bold."

I didn't agree. I shook my head. "I didn't go and see the manager, not because I'm timid, but because I feel I make enough money. So it doesn't bother me that I make less than you."

Lü Qianjin had a good long chuckle after hearing that. "You're incredible," he said.

Lü Qianjin is a good friend. He's always got my interests at heart. After the factory built a new block of housing, he came to give me more advice. "Yang Gao, have you seen? That new apartment building is finally completed. It took a full three years to build it, damn it. We need to go and see the manager and demand that he assigns us new housing. What you have to realize is that after this housing is allocated there won't be any new construction for another ten years, so we have to get our hands on an apartment now, no matter what it takes."

"What do you mean, 'no matter what it takes'?" I asked.

"Starting today," he said, "I'm sleeping at the manager's place."

Lü Qianjin was as good as his word. At nightfall he went off cheerfully to the manager's house, holding a quilt in his arms. Lü Qianjin spent only three nights there before he came into possession of the key to a new apartment. He waved the key in my face. "See this? This is a key! This is the key to my new apartment."

I took Lü Qianjin's key in my hand and inspected it. It was a new key, sure enough. "When you went to the manager's house with a quilt in your arms, what did the manager say?" I asked.

"What did the manager say?" Lü Qianjin thought for a moment and shook his head. "I forget what he said exactly. All I remember is what I said to him. I said that my apartment was too small, that there was no room for me to sleep, so I was moving to his house for the night . . ."

I interrupted him. "Your apartment is bigger than everybody else's. How could you say you have no room to sleep?"

"That's called tactics," said Lü Qianjin. "I put it that way so the manager would be clear that if he didn't give me a new apartment I would stay on at his place. Actually, he knows perfectly well I have a large apartment, but he gave me this key all the same."

After that, Lü Qianjin said to me, "Yang Gao, I'll tell you what to do. Starting today, take all the trash you collect when sweeping the workshop floor and dump it outside the factory manager's apartment. Within three days, the manager will put a new key in your hands."

Saying this, he dangled his key in front of my eyes. "A key just as new as this one."

I shook my head. "Although my apartment's small, there's

plenty of space for my mother and me. I don't need a new apartment."

When he heard me say that, Lü Qianjin clapped me on the shoulder and chuckled. "You're still a sissy, just like your dad."

6

They all said my father was a coward. They said he never got mad at anybody and never raised his voice, even when others stuck their fingers in his face. They could grab him by the lapels of his jacket and hurl abuse at him, but he would never say a word of protest. They said he would bow and scrape to everyone he met, that his face would be wreathed in smiles even if he ran into a beggar who wanted to cadge a meal off him. Anyone else, they said, would send the beggar packing with a kick up his ass, but my father would wine him and dine him, a smile glued on his face the whole time. They told all these stories about my father being a timid creature, rounding them off with commentary on how he didn't smoke and didn't drink.

What they didn't know was that my father looked really fine sitting in his truck. When my father walked toward his Liberation truck, his footsteps resounded with a louder ring than usual and his arms would swing in a wider arc. He would open the door, sit himself down in the cab, and slowly don a pair of white cotton gloves. He would lay his gloved hands on the steering wheel and his foot would press down on the accelerator, and off he would go in his Liberation truck.

They said my father never dared to curse anyone, not even his own wife and child, and they were quite right there—my father never cursed my mother and he never cursed me. But when my father was speeding down the highway in his truck, he did stick his head out the window and shout at pedestrians, "Are you trying to get killed?"

That's when I was sitting in the cab next to him. I was watching the leaves and branches of trees as they flitted past the truck window, watching the road ahead as it glinted in the sunlight. I had a commanding view of the pedestrians who appeared on either side of the highway, and when one of them made a move as if about to cross the road, my father would shout, "Are you trying to get yourself killed?"

My father would turn his head and glance at me. His eyes gleamed with the confidence of a man who was in complete control. "Yang Gao," he would say, "keep a good look out and next time I'll let you be the one to shout."

So then I kept my eyes peeled, watching people walk by the roadside. I saw somebody up ahead begin to cross, only to change his mind and return to the shoulder. I gripped the window frame with both hands and my mouth opened, but no words came out. I was too afraid.

"There's nothing to be afraid of," my father said. "There's no way he can catch up with us."

I watched as our truck roared past. The man quickly became just a tiny figure receding in the distance, and I knew that my father was right—people on the road could not possibly catch up with us, and I could shout at them without the slightest scruple. I put my hands on the window jamb once again, and carefully surveyed the people walking by the side of the road. When another person tried to cross, I felt my body quivering all over and I gave a feeble shout: "Are you trying to get your-self killed?"

"Not loud enough," my father said. "You need to shout louder than that."

In the rearview mirror I could see how the truck quickly left the man behind, and I shouted with all my might, "Are you try-ing to get yourself killed?"

Then I set back against the seat. I felt utterly drained. My father was laughing as he held the steering wheel, and after a moment or two I began to laugh myself.

7

I like being with Lü Qianjin, because he's such a daredevil. He's more fearless even than Zhao Qing, Song Hai, Fang Dawei, Hu Qiang, Liu Jisheng, or Xu Hao. Though he's the smallest and skinniest of the lot, he's much the most daring. I often wonder if Lü Qianjin has eyes like a goose, so everybody looks puny in his eyes, so he's afraid of nobody. He has three stab wounds on his face, all from cuts he inflicted on himself with a kitchen cleaver. He ran home after losing a fight, picked up the kitchen cleaver, and then chased after his adversary. When he caught up with him, he cut himself on the face, then raised the cleaver and advanced on his enemy, who took to his heels in fear.

Later, Song Hai and the others said, "Nobody would ever dream of cutting their own face with a cleaver, but Lü Qianjin will. That's why everyone is afraid of him."

"Why did you have to cut your face?" I asked him.

"That was to show the other guy I would stop at nothing," said Lü Qianjin. "You know what they say: 'The timid fear the bold, and the bold fear the reckless.'"

That's when I realized Lü Qianjin was even more daring than the bold—he was reckless. "And what are reckless people afraid of?" I asked him.

"They're not afraid of anything."

There he was wrong. Reckless people actually have moments when they're scared too, and Lü Qianjin is a case in point. There was one night—and very late it was—one night when Lü Qianjin and I had both been working on the final shift of the day. I left the plant ahead of him, and walked as far as a street that had no lights. It began to rain, so I took shelter under the eaves of a house and stood there in the dark for some time. Then I heard footsteps approaching, but I couldn't see who it was—all I could make out vaguely was a low silhouette. As the figure came closer I could see he had a coat draped over his shoulders and was walking toward me with his head down. As he passed he gave a cough, and right away I knew who it was. It was Lü Qianjin. Because he had a cold he had been coughing the whole day through. When he coughed it sounded even more disgusting than the sound of someone throwing up—it was as though his throat was clogged with sand. He gave a drawn-out, hacking cough as he walked past.

By this time I must have been standing under the ink-black eaves for a good ten minutes. Although the rain didn't get my face wet, it had soaked my shoes right through. I was so pleased to see Lü Qianjin come along that I darted out and put my arms around him. I felt his body contract and heard him scream out in panic, "I'm a man! I'm a man! I'm a man!"

I'd never heard a scream like that—it was a bit like the crow a rooster makes, not at all like the kind of shout you'd expect to hear from Lü Qianjin. He had never spoken or shouted in that tone of voice before. He burst free from my grasp and started running for all he was worth, and in the blink of an eye he disappeared around the corner. He ran away so quickly, I didn't even have time to tell him it was me. As soon as I put my arms around him, he screamed, and it startled me so much that by the time I had recovered from my surprise he had already vanished into the distance.

That night I puzzled over it, but I just couldn't figure out why he shouted "I'm a man." I knew he was a man, obviously— what I didn't understand was why he had to say so. He didn't need to say that for me to know he was a man. It wasn't until the next day, at Song Hai's place, when I was sitting around with Lü Qianjin, Zhao Qing, Song Hai, Fang Dawei, Hu Qiang, Liu Jisheng, and Xu Hao, that I learned why Lü Qianjin had screamed the way he did.

Lü Qianjin was sitting opposite me. With a cigarette in one hand and a cup of tea in the other, he said, "Somebody tried to rape me last night."

"A woman tried to rape you?" asked Song Hai.

"A man," said Lü Qianjin. "He took me for a woman . . ."

"How could he mistake you for a woman?" they asked.

"I had this bright-colored coat over my shoulders," said Lü Qianjin. "It was raining when I got off work, so I grabbed the coat of one of the women in the workshop and threw it over my head. I went out the gate and got as far as Army Emulation Road. That fucking road hasn't got a single streetlamp, and as soon as I started walking down the road, the rapist jumped on me from behind and put his arms around me . . ."

"So that's why you screamed 'I'm a man!'" I cried out in delight. "It's because you had a woman's coat on your shoulders . . ."

They interrupted me. "What did you do when he put his arms around you?" they asked Lü Qianjin.

He gave me a look. "I grabbed his two hands, and with a quick flick of my waist I threw him like a sack to the ground . . ."

"And then?"

"Then . . ." Lü Qianjin gave me another look. "I stuck my foot in his mouth and said, 'I'm a man.'"

Having heard what Lü Qianjin had to say, Song Hai and the others turned and looked at me, as though they recalled what I had just said. Song Hai pointed at me. "What was it he said just now?"

I laughed. So they went back to quizzing Lü Qianjin: "What then?"

"Then," Lü Qianjin continued, his eyes fixed on me, "I kicked him a couple of times, and then I picked him up and punched him in the face a couple of times, and then . . . and then . . ."

When Lü Qianjin saw I was laughing all the more heartily, he glared at me. "Yang Gao, what's so funny?"

"Actually," I said, "I had no idea you were wearing a woman's coat. It was so dark, there was no way I could tell what you were wearing."

Lü Qianjin turned pale. Song Hai and the others looked at me. "What did you say?" they asked.

I pointed at myself. "It was me who put my arms around him last night," I said.

They were stunned. I looked at Lü Qianjin. "Last night you

ran so fast I didn't have the chance to tell you it was me. You ran out of sight in a flash."

Lü Qianjin sprang to his feet, his face livid. He came up to me, raised his hand, and gave me two resounding slaps across the ears that left my head spinning. Then he picked me up by the lapels of my jacket and pulled me out of my chair. First he thrust his knee into my belly, so hard my stomach felt it had been hit by a sledgehammer, and then he planted a fist in my chest, so fiercely it knocked the breath out of me.

8

Afterward, I dragged myself up off the floor. I left Song Hai's house and slowly followed Liberation Road until I reached Sunnyside Bridge. I stopped there for a while and leaned against the balustrade; the midday sun beat down so strongly I could hardly open my eyes. My body was still aching. I heard a boat pass under the bridge; it made a lapping sound as it cut its way through the water. I thought of my father, who died the year I turned twelve. I thought of the summer he died, of the Liberation truck he drove that summer and that battered old tractor.

My father let me sit in the cab of his truck. He was going to take me to Shanghai, to the big city. My father's truck sped along the summer highway. The wind, warmed by the sun, ruffled my hair as I sat there in the cab and made my shirt flap. "Why don't you close your eyes?" I said to my father.

"You can't close your eyes when driving," he said.

"Why not?" I said. "Why can't you?"

"Do you see the tractor up ahead?" my father said.

I saw a tractor creeping along, with a dozen or so farm workers sitting in the cart it was pulling. They were all stripped to the waist, and they looked black and shiny, like loaches. "I see it," I said.

"If I was to close my eyes," said my father, "we would run right into the tractor, and the impact would kill us."

"All I want is for you to just close them for a moment," I said. "If you can just do that, then I can tell Lü Qianjin and the others about it. I can tell them you have the nerve to drive with your eyes closed."

"Okay, I'll just close them for a moment," said my father. "Watch my eyes. I am going to close them on the count of three. One, two, three . . ."

My father closed his eyes. I saw it for myself—his eyes, for that moment, were completely shut. When he opened them again, our truck was about to crash into the tractor and the tractor was veering off to the left in alarm. My father jerked the steering wheel as sharply as he could and our truck just managed to scrape past.

I saw those dark, loachlike men in the cart shake their fists at us, and I knew they must be cursing. That's when my father stuck out his head and shouted back, "Are you trying to get yourselves killed?"

My father turned to me and gave a smile of satisfaction. I smiled too, as our truck raced on along the summer highway and leaves and branches flitted past. I saw fields full of crops, a patch of this and a patch of that, houses and winding rivers, and people making their way along the paths between the fields.

But then my father's truck broke down. He got out, opened the hood, and began to repair his Liberation. I stayed put in the cab. I wanted to watch my father as he worked, but the raised hood blocked my view and I had to content myself with listening to him making the repairs. He tapped away at things under the hood.

Time passed; finally my father jumped down and slammed the hood shut. He came round and fished out a cloth from under my seat, rubbed the oil off his hands, and then walked round to the other side. Just as he opened his door and was about to climb in, the tractor we had passed earlier rolled up, disgorging the men as dark as loaches, who made a beeline for our truck.

My father watched white-knuckled as they marched over. Hands grabbed his shirt collar—three hands, at the very least. "Who is trying to get killed?" I heard them ask. "Is it us, or is it you?"

My father said nothing. They dragged him to the middle of the road, and I saw their hands reach into my father's trousers, take out his cash, and transfer it to their own pockets. After that, their fists started landing on his face, and the twelve of them together beat him up and knocked him to the ground.

In the truck, I was crying. I couldn't see my father, because he was completely surrounded. I wept and wailed as they kicked him. Only when they drifted away did I see him curled up on the ground, as though hugging himself. I was crying fit to burst, because I saw four of the men had opened their flies and were pissing on my father as he lay there, on his face and his legs and his chest. I sobbed and moaned, and through a veil of tears I saw them walk toward the tractor and climb back onto the trailer. The tractor began to chug, and off they went.

My father clambered to his feet and stood stock-still for a minute or two, his body stooped, as I wept and wailed. He turned around and came back to the truck, and when he opened the door I could see that his face was caked with blood and dirt and his hair and clothes were wet. He panted as he climbed into the cab. I was crying so much, my body was trembling all over. He reached over and rubbed my face with his grimy hand, lightly rubbing my face until my tears were dry. He laid his hands on the steering wheel and gazed at the tractor as it drove off into the distance. After a moment, he drew out his tea mug from its place by his feet and handed it to me. "Yang Gao, I'm thirsty," he said. "Go down to the river and fill this up with water."

Still sobbing, I took the mug from his hand, opened the door, climbed out, and walked down to the bank. I took a look back at my father. He was watching me with tears in his eyes. I went down to the river.

When I stood up after filling the mug, my father's truck had begun to roll forward. I ran up the bank as fast as I could, spilling the water on the ground, but the truck just kept on moving. I stood and wailed at the side of the road, shouting desperately at the departing truck, "Don't leave me! Don't leave me!"

I ran after the truck, crying and screaming. I thought my father didn't want me anymore, I thought he was deserting me. The truck was moving at full speed now, and I watched as it gained on the tractor. Then I heard a colossal roar and all I could see was a huge cloud of dust; black smoke was beginning to rise.

I stood rooted to the spot for some minutes. Vehicles had pulled over by the crash site, and passengers got out and gathered round. I went on walking—it was a long way ahead—and it was almost dark by the time I reached my father's truck. Its front end had caved in and the door on the driver's side was twisted out of shape; he lay sprawled over the steering wheel and his head was covered with broken glass. The steering column had punctured his shirt, punctured his chest; blood had stained his body red. The men had been thrown from the tractor: some were groaning, while others lay motionless. Sparrows were strewn everywhere, carpeting the ground as thickly as the vegetables in the fields. I realized they must have been killed by the sheer impact of that tremendous roar. They had been perched on a tree as happy as can be, but my father's truck collided with the tractor and suddenly that was the end of them.

9

I left Sunnyside Bridge and went home. My mother was not there. The clothes she had washed that morning had been hung out to dry on the bamboo rails by the window. I saw they were dry, so I collected and folded them and put them away. I swept one more time the floor my mother had swept that morning, wiped the table she had wiped, put in order the shoes she had straightened, and filled up her cup with water. Then I took the cleaver from the kitchen and went out the door.

As I walked toward Lü Qianjin's house, the cleaver in my hand, I passed Song Hai's place. Song Hai stopped me. "Yang

Gao, where are you off to? What are you doing with that cleaver in your hand?"

"I'm going to Lü Qianjin's house," I said. "I'm going to carve him up."

Song Hai laughed. I heard his voice behind me. "Fang Dawei, do you see this? See the cleaver Yang Gao is holding? He says he's going to carve up Lü Qianjin."

Fang Dawei was coming my way. Hearing this, he stopped. "Are you really going to carve him up?"

I nodded. "I really am."

Fang Dawei laughed just as loud and long as Song Hai. "He says he's really going to carve up Lü Qianjin."

"That's right. That's what he says."

They laughed, and fell in behind me. They said they wanted to see with their own eyes how I was going to carve up Lü Qianjin. So there I was walking on in front and they were walking behind. When we passed Liu Jisheng's apartment, Song Hai and Fang Dawei shouted out, "Liu Jisheng! Liu Jisheng!"

Liu Jisheng appeared in his doorway. He looked at us. "What's up?" he said.

"Yang Gao is going to carve up Lü Qianjin," they told him. "Don't you want to get a view of the action?"

Liu Jisheng looked at me in amazement. "You're going to carve up Lü Qianjin?"

I nodded. "That's right," I said. "That's just what I'm going to do."

Liu Jisheng laughed, just like Song Hai and Fang Dawei. "Are you planning to kill him? Or just do him some damage?"

"Maybe not kill him," I said, "but at least leave him in pretty bad shape."

Hearing this, they laughed so hard they had to put their

hands on their bellies. It was a mystery to me why they found this so funny. "How come you guys are so pleased to hear that I'm going to carve up Lü Qianjin?" I said. "You're his friends, after all."

They laughed so much they squatted down on their haunches, and their laughter gradually turned to titters, a bit like the sound crickets make. I ignored them and went on ahead by myself. When I passed Hu Qiang's place, I heard Song Hai and the others shout, "Hu Qiang! Hu Qiang! Hu Qiang!"

They were going to follow me the whole way, I realized. The result was that when I reached Lü Qianjin's house, there were five people with me: Song Hao, Fang Dawei, Liu Jisheng, Hu Qiang, and Xu Hao. Laughing gaily, they pushed me inside.

Lü Qianjin sat at the table clutching a big slice of watermelon; some seeds were stuck to his cheeks. When he raised his head to look at us, he saw what I had in my hand. "What are you doing with that cleaver?" he mumbled, his mouth full of melon.

"Yang Gao is going to carve you up with it!" Song Hai and the others said gleefully.

Lü Qianjin's eyes widened. He looked at me, then at Song Hai and the others. "What did you say?"

Song Hai and company burst out laughing. "Lü Qianjin," they said, "death's staring you in the face, and here you are eating watermelon. You'd better stop. The melon you're eating won't have time to turn into shit, because you're about to die. Don't you see the cleaver in Yang Gao's hand?"

Lü Qianjin put down the watermelon. He pointed at me, then at his nose. "You're saying he wants to carve me up?"

Song Hai and company nodded. "That's right!" they said.

Lü Qianjin wiped his mouth with his hand and pointed at me a second time. "You're telling me Yang Gao wants to carve me up with that cleaver?"

They nodded again. "You've got it!"

Lü Qianjin looked at me and burst out laughing, along with Song Hai and company. That's when I spoke up. "Lü Qianjin," I said. "You beat me up. You slapped me in the face, you punched me in the chest, and you kicked me in the stomach and kicked me on the knees, and my face and my chest and my stomach and my knees are still sore. When you were hitting me, I never once hit back. That wasn't because I was afraid of you, it was because I didn't know what to do. Now I know what to do: I want a tooth for a tooth. I'm going to carve you up with this cleaver."

I raised the cleaver to show Lü Qianjin, and to show Song Hai and the others too.

They looked at the cleaver in my upraised hand; their mouths opened and laughter came out. I thought to myself, What's the matter with them? Why are they laughing so hard? So I asked them, I said, "What's so funny? What are you so happy about? Lü Qianjin, why are you laughing too? I've got an idea why Song Hai and the rest of them are laughing, but I can't understand why you think it's so funny."

They just laughed all the harder. Lü Qianjin fell on the table, he was laughing so much. Song Hai and Fang Dawei stood next to him, one hand on their bellies and one hand on his shoulder. My ears were buzzing with the sound of their laughter. I stood there with the cleaver in my hand and didn't know what to do. I watched as they laughed, watched as they gradually stopped laughing and wiped away their tears. Then

Song Hai pressed Lü Qianjin's head down on the table. "You need to offer Yang Gao your neck."

Lü Qianjin raised his head and shoved Song Hai's hand aside. "No way! No way am I going to offer him my neck."

Song Hai persisted. "Come on, give him your neck. If you don't do that, he won't know what to do."

Fang Dawei and company added their comments. "Lü Qianjin, if you don't give him your neck, it won't be any fun."

"Fuck this," said Lü Qianjin. Then with a laugh he laid his head on the table. Liu Jisheng and the rest pushed me over next to Lü Qianjin, and Song Hai took my hand and guided the cleaver to Lü Qianjin's neck. When the cleaver made contact with his skin, his neck contracted, and he sniggered. "The cleaver's making my neck all itchy," he said.

I noticed some pimples on Lü Qianjin's sunburned neck. "You've got a lot of spots," I said. "Your system is out of whack. You must not have been eating enough vegetables lately."

"I haven't eaten any vegetables at all," he said.

"If you don't fancy vegetables, then watermelon will do just as well," I said.

"Yang Gao, cut the crap," Song Hai and the others said. "Weren't you planning to carve up Lü Qianjin? Now you have his neck right underneath your cleaver and we want to watch how you do it."

It was true. Lü Qianjin's neck was at the mercy of my cleaver. All I needed to do was to raise my arm, chop, and his neck would be severed. But when I saw Song Hai and the others again killing themselves laughing, I couldn't help thinking that the prospect of seeing me cut his head off was what made them so happy, and I began to feel distressed on Lü Qianjin's account. "They're supposed to be your friends," I said. "But if they were really your friends, they wouldn't be so happy. They should be trying to talk me out of it. They should be pulling me away. But look at them—they're looking forward to me cutting your head off."

Hearing this, they laughed all the louder. "See, there they go again," I said to Lü Qianjin.

He was laughing too, still with his head against the table. "You're right," he said. "They're not true friends of mine. But then neither are you. If you were really my friend, you wouldn't be about to cut my head off with a cleaver."

This made me uneasy. "The only reason I'm doing this," I said, "is because you beat me up. I wouldn't be doing it otherwise."

"I just hit you a couple of times, that's all," Lü Qianjin said, "but here you are cutting me up with a cleaver. You're forgetting how good I was to you in the past."

This made me think. I recalled things that had happened earlier, times when Lü Qianjin had helped me out, when he'd got into a fight or a row with someone on my account, and lots of other things, but now I was trying to cut him up. Although he had given me a beating, he was still my friend. I put the cleaver to one side. "Lü Qianjin," I said, "I am not going to cut you up after all."

Lü Qianjin lifted his head off the table and gave his neck a rub. He looked at Song Hai and the others and laughed, and they looked at him and laughed.

"Although I'm not going to cut you up," I went on, "I can't just leave it like this. You slapped me and kicked me all over the place. I'm going to give you a slap now, and we'll call it quits."

I reached out and gave him a box on the ear. When people heard the whack of my hand hitting Lü Qianjin's face, their laughter evaporated. I saw Lü Qianjin's eyes widen. He pointed at me and cursed. "What the hell do you think you're doing!"

He knocked over the chair and delivered four slaps to my face, hitting me so hard that my head lolled and my eyes went blurry, and then he punched me fiercely in the chest, so hard my lungs wheezed. I fell to the ground, and he kicked me in the belly, so hard my stomach churned. His foot delivered a series of kicks to my legs, hard enough to break my bones. As I lay on the floor, I heard a buzz of conversation, though I couldn't make out what they were saying. All I felt was waves of pain from head to toe, as though my body was being wrung out like a wet towel.

THEIR SON

At five o'clock on a Saturday afternoon, several hundred workers crowded around the main entrance to the machine factory, waiting for the bell that would mark the end of their shift. The metal gate, still tightly shut, clanged as the people in front banged against it, while a buzz of conversation rose up from the people behind, punctuated by shouts here and there. As they awaited release, the workers were like livestock trapped behind bars, idly clustered in the dimming light of dusk, crowded together in the howling wind. The large windows in the factory behind them were already shrouded in darkness, and the desolate scene was enlivened only by the clouds of dust that swirled around the workshops.

Shi Zhikang, a man of fifty-one, stood in the front row in his military overcoat, directly facing the crack between the two leaves of the steel gate. The icy wind blew in through the narrow gap and onto his face, making him feel as though his nose was shrinking.

Next to him stood the old gatekeeper, his bald head flushed by the cold. Over a thick padded jacket he wore a faded boiler suit; the end of a large key projected from his chest pocket. People were yelling at him to open the gate, but he might as well have been deaf. He looked from side to side, and every time someone directed an impatient comment his way he would turn his head and look in the other direction. Only when the bell rang did the old man finally take the key from his pocket, while the people in the front row took a step back to give him room. As he moved forward, he made a point of thrusting his elbows behind him and put the key in the hole only when his arms met no resistance. .

Shi Zhikang was the first to make it out the gate. He set off rapidly along the road to his right, planning to walk to the stop before the factory and catch the trolleybus there, to avoid the scrum outside the gate. At least forty workers would try to push and shove their way onto the trolleybus, although it would already be full of passengers by the time it reached the factory.

As he walked, Shi Zhikang thought about those forty workmates, imagining how they would cluster around the bus stop just as they had crammed in front of the gate. There would be a dozen hefty young men and at least a dozen women, three of whom had started work the same year as him. All three had medical conditions now: one had a ropy heart and the other two had kidney problems.

As he was thinking about that, the bus stop came into view, and at the same time he saw a trolleybus coming his way, so he took his hands out of his pockets and ran, arriving at the stop just as the bus pulled in. People were already waiting there in three clusters and, as the bus slowed down, the clusters moved to position themselves in line with the bus's three doors. When the bus stopped, the clusters became stationary. The doors opened and passengers squeezed out in a tight, solid stream like toothpaste from a tube, and then, in a dense mass of limbs, people piled on.

By the time the trolley approached the entrance to Shi Zhikang's factory, he had already pushed his way into the middle of the bus, and his arms were wedged vertically into the gaps left by bodies pressed up against him. The bus didn't stop outside the factory but drove right on past. Of the forty workers who had been waiting there, only five or six were left, along with seven or eight people he didn't recognize, so one or two other buses must have come along. The three women had evidently been unable to cram aboard, for they still were waiting at the stop, the one with the bad heart in the middle, the two with kidney disease on either side. They stood in a tight clump in their dumpy padded coats, each with a black woolen scarf around her neck. The chill wind blew their hair every which way, and the deepening darkness blurred their features, as though their faces had been charred by fire. As his trolley passed them, Shi Zhikang noticed how their heads turned to follow it. They watched as the bus he was on sailed away from them.

After nine stops Shi Zhikang got off the trolleybus and walked back thirty yards to another stop, where he would board another bus. By this time the sky was completely dark; the streetlamps cast only a feeble glow and it was more the bright lights of the stores on either side of the street that illuminated the sidewalk and the area around the bus stop. Many people were already waiting, and those closest to the front were practically standing in the middle of the street. As Shi Zhikang made his way into the crowd, a minibus came along and, when the door opened, a young man with a canvas satchel hanging from his neck poked his head out and yelled: "Two yuan, two yuan . . ."

Two men and a woman boarded the minibus, as the conductor continued to shout, "Two yuan . . ."

At this point a bus turned a corner away in the distance

and came into view. Seeing it, the conductor quickly ducked back inside and the minibus accelerated away from the waiting throng, as the bus rumbled toward them.

Shi Zhikang swiftly pushed his way to the front and spread his arms a little, pressing backward as the bus approached, pushing the people behind him back onto the sidewalk. As the front door of the bus slipped past, he monitored the bus's speed and calculated that he should be perfectly in line for the middle door. But what happened was that the bus came to an abrupt stop, leaving him a yard or two away from his target door. He'd lost his position in the front row, and now he found himself on the outer edge of the crowd.

When the door opened, only three people got off. Shi Zhikang took a couple of steps into the crowd and thrust his arms into a tiny gap left by the people in front. As he pushed his way forward, he made good use of the upper-body strength acquired in his long years as a fitter. He steadily widened the gap, then squeezed into the space created, and began to work on opening a gap farther ahead.

Shi Zhikang plowed his way through the line and launched himself into the space by the door, exploiting the impetus of the people pressing from behind. Just as he planted one foot on the step of the bus, someone grabbed the collar of his overcoat and dragged him backward. He landed heavily on the ground and his head hit a leg. The leg retaliated with a kick, and he looked up to find a young woman glaring at him.

By the time Shi Zhikang was back on his feet, the doors had closed and the bus was beginning to move off. A woman's handbag was trapped in the door, leaving a corner of the bag and part of the strap sticking outside, so that it swayed back and forth with the motion of the bus. He turned around, determined to find out who had pulled him back. Two youths about the same age as his son were watching him with a cold glint in their eyes. He looked at them and at others who had failed to squeeze onto the bus. Some returned his gaze, some did not. He was tempted to let off a swearword or two, but thought better of it.

Later, two buses arrived at the same time, and Shi Zhikang boarded the second. Today he did not get off at the stop closest to his home, but two stops earlier, where a man with a flat-bed cart sold bean curd that tasted better than what you could buy in the shops. Shi Zhikang's wife, who worked in a textile mill, had asked him to pick up a couple of pounds on his way home from work, because today was Saturday and their son, a junior in college, was coming home for the weekend.

After buying the bean curd, Shi Zhikang did not try to catch another bus and simply walked the rest of the way home. It was almost seven o'clock, but there was no sign of his wife. This upset him. His wife should have got off work at four thirty, and she did not have such a long commute. Normally his wife would have dinner practically ready by this time, but today he had to set to on an empty stomach, washing vegetables and slicing meat.

His wife, Li Xiulan, came in the door with a bag of fish. "Have you washed your hands?" was the first thing she said.

Shi Zhikang was not in a good mood, so he answered curtly. "Can't you see my hands are wet?"

"Did you use soap?" she asked. "There's flu going around, and pneumonia too. You need to wash your hands with soap as soon as you get home."

Shi Zhikang snorted dismissively. "Then shouldn't you come home sooner?"

Li Xiulan dumped the two fish in the sink. She told Shi Zhikang they cost her only three yuan. "They were the last two. He wanted five yuan, but I wouldn't go higher than three."

"Does it take so long to buy a couple of dead fish?"

"They haven't been dead long." She showed him the gills: "See, the cheeks are still red."

"It's you I'm talking about." He raised his voice as he pointed at his watch. "It's after seven already!"

Her tone also went up a register. "So what? What's the big deal about me coming home late? Every day you get back later than I do—do I complain?"

"Do I finish work before you do? Is my factory closer to home than yours?"

"I fell down," said Li Xiulan.

She flung the fish back in the sink and stamped into the living room. "I fell off the bus," she said, "and it was ages before I could stand up again. I had to sit there on the side of the road for thirty or forty minutes. I practically froze to death."

Shi Zhikang set down the cleaver he'd been using to slice the meat and walked over to her: "You fell? So did I—someone tugged my collar."

He didn't finish the story, for now she had rolled up her trouser leg and he could see there was a bruise as big as an egg on her knee. He bent down to touch it. "How did it happen?"

"When I was getting off the bus, there were too many people behind me. They pushed so hard I lost my balance."

Just then their son arrived home, dressed in a red down jacket. Seeing his mother had suffered a fall, he bent down like his father had done. "Did you trip?" he asked with concern. Then he took off his jacket. "You should be taking a calcium supplement," he went on. "It's not only babies who need calcium, older people need it too. Every day your bones lose calcium, and that makes you prone to injury . . . If I got pushed off a bus, there's no way I would end up with such a large bruise."

Their son turned on the television and plumped himself down on the sofa. He put on the earphones of his Walkman and began to listen to some music.

"Are you watching TV?" Shi Zhikang asked. "Or listening to the radio?"

His son looked at him, but almost immediately turned away again, not having understood the question. "Have you washed your hands?" his mother asked.

He swiveled his head and removed an earphone from one of his ears. "What did you say?"

"Go and wash your hands," Li Xiulan said. "There's flu going around now and it's easy to pick up germs on the bus. Go wash your hands, and be sure to use soap."

"I don't need to wash my hands." Their son replaced the earphone. "I took a cab."

SHI ZHIKANG COULDN'T GET TO SLEEP that night. For five months now, his wife had been bringing home only a little over a hundred yuan. He was in a better position— four hundred yuan—but still their combined monthly income was less than six hundred. The cost of rice had now risen to one yuan thirty a pound, and pork was twelve yuan a pound— even chili peppers were three yuan a pound. They still gave their son three hundred yuan a month for living expenses all the same, leaving a bit over two hundred for themselves. But this hadn't stopped their son from taking a taxi when he came home on Saturday.

Li Xiulan had not fallen asleep either. She noticed her husband was tossing and turning. "You can't sleep?"

"No."

She turned to face him. "How much do you think our son paid to come home in a taxi?"

"I don't know. I've never taken a taxi." He paused. "I guess it would have cost at least thirty yuan."

"Thirty yuan?" she moaned.

"We sweated blood for this money," he sighed.

They said nothing more. Before long he fell asleep, and soon she was asleep too.

The next morning, their son again put on his earphones and watched TV as he listened to music. Shi Zhikang and Li Xiulan decided to have a good talk with him, so she sat down by his side, while her husband brought a chair over and sat in front of them. "Your mother and I would like to have a chat with you," Shi Zhikang said.

"What about?" Because of the earphones, their son spoke loudly.

"Family matters."

"Go on." He was practically shouting.

Shi Zhikang leaned over and removed his right earphone. "These past few months, we've had a few problems. We didn't want to tell you, for fear of distracting you from your studies . . ."

"What's happened?" Their son removed the other earphone.

"Nothing much," Shi Zhikang said. "Beginning this month, there'll be no more night shift in our factory, and of the three hundred in the workforce, half will be laid off. As far as I'm concerned, it's no big deal—I have skills, the factory still needs me . . . It's more what's happening with your mom. Currently she is just bringing home a bit over one hundred yuan a month. She's due to retire in four years, and if she was to take early retirement, she could get three hundred yuan a month, and that would carry on for three years . . ."

"You get paid more if you take early retirement?"

They nodded. "In that case, why don't you retire?" their son asked.

"Your mother and I are thinking that too," Shi Zhikang said.

"Yeah, retire." Saying this, their son prepared to put his earphones back on. Shi Zhikang threw his wife a glance. "Son," she said, "our family finances aren't what they used to be, and in the future they may be in even poorer shape . . ."

Their son already had one earphone in place. "What was that?" he asked.

"Your mom was saying that the family finances aren't what they used to be," Shi Zhikang said.

"Never mind about that." Their son waved his hand. "State finances aren't what they used to be either."

His parents exchanged glances. "Tell me this," said Shi Zhikang. "Why did you come home in a taxi yesterday?"

Their son looked at them, perplexed. "Why didn't you take a bus?" Shi Zhikang persisted.

"The bus is too crowded."

"Too crowded?"

Shi Zhikang pointed at Li Xiulan. "Your mom and I cram

ourselves onto buses every day of the week. How can a young guy like you be afraid of crowded buses?"

"It's not the pushing that's the problem, it's the smell." Their son frowned. "I really hate smelling other people's body odor. In buses, everybody's jostling you, forcing you to smell their stink. It's so packed and stuffy, even perfume smells bad. Plus, there are people letting off farts as well . . .

"I feel like throwing up every time I get on a bus," he concluded.

"Throwing up?" Li Xiulan was shocked. "Son, are you ill?"

"No, of course not."

She looked at Shi Zhikang. "Could it be stomach trouble?"

Her husband nodded. "Have you got a bellyache?" he asked.

"There's nothing wrong with me." Their son was getting impatient.

"What's your appetite like these days?" Li Xiulan asked.

"I don't have any stomach trouble!" their son yelled.

"Are you sleeping all right?" Shi Zhikang asked. He turned to Li Xiulan: "If you don't get enough sleep, it'll make you feel nauseous."

Their son stretched out all ten fingers: "I sleep ten hours a day."

Li Xiulan was still anxious. "Son, you'd better go to the hospital for a checkup."

"I told you, there's nothing wrong with me." Their son jumped to his feet. "This is all about me having taken a taxi for once, isn't it?" he cried. "Well, I won't be taking any more taxis . . ."

"Son, we're not bothered about the taxi fare," said Shi Zhikang. "We're thinking of you. You'll be starting a job

soon, and when you rely on your own salary you'll understand that money doesn't come easily and you have to budget
accordingly . . ."

"That's right." Li Xiulan went on. "We never said you
couldn't take a taxi."

"In the future there's no way I'll be taking taxis." Their son
sat back down on the sofa. "In the future I will drive my own
car," he explained. He put the earphones over his ears. "My
classmates take taxis all the time."

"His classmates take taxis all the time," Li Xiulan repeated,
looking at her husband. Seeing him nod, she went on. "If other
people's sons can take taxis, why shouldn't ours?"

"I never said he couldn't," said Shi Zhikang.

Their son was maybe now listening to one of his favorite
songs, for he was rocking his head back and forth and mouth-
ing some lyrics. They looked at each other and smiled as they
studied his contented air. Maybe the future would bring more
and more difficulties, but this did not distress them unduly, for
they could see their son was now his own man.

THE SKIPPING-AND-STEPPING GAME

In a street-corner vending kiosk that sells groceries and fruit, a tired and sagging face spends year after year in the company of cookies, instant noodles, candies, tobacco, and cans of soda, like an old calendar stuck on the wall. A body and limbs are attached to this face, along with the name Lin Deshun.

Lin Deshun sat in a wheelchair, looking through the tiny window in front of him at the street outside. A young couple was standing on the sidewalk opposite, with a little boy between them who looked to be about six or seven. The boy was wearing a thick down jacket and a red hat, and a scarf just as red was tied around his neck. Although it was now the season of spring balm and flower blossoms, the boy was dressed for winter's cold.

They were outside a hospital, and stood together quietly amid the commotion of people going in and out. The father, hands in his pockets, gazed intently toward the entrance, and his wife, her right hand holding the boy's left hand, watched with equal concentration. It was only the boy whose eyes were turned in the direction of the street. With his mother clasping his hand, he had to twist himself around to look, but his eyes dwelled avidly on the scene before him. His head was continually on the move and often he would raise his free hand to point something out to them. It was clear there was no end of things he wanted to tell his parents, but they just stood there like statues.

After a little while, the parents led the boy a few steps closer to the entrance and Lin Deshun saw that a rather plump nurse was approaching them. They came to a stop and began to talk, but the boy maintained his sideways stance, his eyes glued to the street.

The nurse finished speaking and went back into the hospital. The boy's parents turned around and, taking the boy by the hand, cautiously crossed the street and arrived outside Lin Deshun's kiosk. The father released his grip on his son's hand, walked up to the window, and took a look inside. Lin Deshun saw a face covered with stubble, a pair of eyes swollen from lack of sleep, and the grubby collar of a white shirt. "Can I help you?" he asked.

The man looked at the tangerines on display right in front of him. "Give me a tangerine," he said.

"One tangerine?" Lin Deshun thought he had misheard.

The father reached out a hand and took a tangerine. "How much?"

Lin Deshun thought for a moment. "Let's say twenty fen."

When the man's hand laid twenty fen on the counter, Lin Deshun noticed several threads from his sweater protruding from his sleeve.

After buying the tangerine, the father turned around to find that mother and son were holding hands and playing a game on the sidewalk. The boy was trying to step on his mother's foot and she kept skipping out of the way. "You can't get me, you can't get me . . . ," she would call.

"I'm going to get you, I'm going to get you . . . ," the boy cried.

The father stood to one side, tangerine in hand, watching their boisterous game, until finally the son stepped on his mother's foot and gave a triumphant cry: "I got you!" That was when the father said, "Come and have some tangerine." Lin Deshun now got a clear view of the boy's face. When he raised his head to take the fruit, Lin Deshun saw a pair of luminous dark eyes, but the boy's face was frighteningly pale— even his lips were practically as white as chalk. Now the family was just as quiet as they had been when standing on the other side of the street. The boy peeled the tangerine and began to eat it as he walked away, parents on either side.

Lin Deshun knew they must have come to register their child as an in-patient, but today no bed was available, so now they were going back home.

Lin Deshun saw them again the following morning, standing outside the hospital just like the day before. What was different was that this time only the father was gazing in the direction of the hospital, while mother and son, hand in hand, were happily playing their skipping-and-stepping game. From his side of the street, Lin Deshun could hear them calling:

"You can't get me, you can't get me . . ."

"I'm going to get you, I'm going to get you . . ."

Their cries were full of delight, as if they were on a park lawn, not by the hospital gate. The boy's voice rang clear, instantly recognizable amid the entrance hubbub and the clamor of vehicles in the street.

"I'm going to get you, I'm going to get you . . ."

Then there emerged the same plump nurse as the day before, and the skipping-and-stepping game came to an end. Parents and son followed the nurse into the hospital.

It was another morning, about a week later, that Lin Deshun saw the young couple emerge from the hospital. They were walking slowly; the husband had his arm around his wife, and her head rested on his shoulder. Slowly, quietly, they crossed the street and came toward Lin Deshun's kiosk, then stopped. The husband disengaged his arm and walked over. He placed his unshaven face close up to the window and looked inside. "Do you want a tangerine?" Lin Deshun asked.

"Give me a bun," the man said.

Lin Deshun gave him a bun, and after taking the money from him inquired: "Is the boy all right?"

The man had turned to leave, but on hearing this he swiveled round and looked at Lin Deshun. "The boy?"

His eyes rested on Lin Deshun's face for a moment. "He died," he said in a low voice.

He rejoined his wife and gave her the bun: "Have some of this."

His wife's head was bowed, as though she were looking at her feet. Her loose hair concealed her face, and she shook her head. "I don't want it."

"Have a little, at least," her husband persisted.

"I don't want it." She shook her head again. "You have it."

After a moment of hesitation, he clumsily bit off a mouthful of bun. He extended his arm toward his wife, and she compliantly laid her head on his shoulder. He put his arm around her, and slowly and quietly the two of them walked off in a westerly direction.

Lin Deshun could no longer see them, for the merchandise blocked his view, so he went on looking across the street at the entrance to the hospital. He noticed the sky had darkened, and looking up he knew it was about to rain. He didn't like rain. On an evening many years ago, when it was pelting down, he had rushed up the stairs to close the windows, clutching his overcoat; halfway up he suddenly lost his footing, and from then on he was paralyzed. Now he sits in a wheelchair.

Why Do I Have to Get Married?

When I decided to visit those friends of mine, I was
with my mother, arranging things in the kitchen of
the new apartment, and my father was calling me again and
again from his study, wanting me to help him organize his huge
pile of musty books. I'm their only son. The kitchen needed
me, the study needed me, both my parents needed me, but
there was just one of me. "Better get a cleaver and chop me
into two," I said.

"Take this box of kitchenware we don't use and put it up
there out of the way," my mother said.

"Come and help me move this bookcase," my father called
from the study.

"Better get a cleaver and chop me into two," I kept on
repeating, while I put the box of kitchenware away for my
mother and helped my father shift the bookcase. After reposi-
tioning the furniture, I became Father's property. He grabbed
me by the arm, wanting me to take books that he'd sorted out
and set them down row by row on the bookcase. My mother
called to me from the kitchen, wanting me to bring down the
box of unused kitchenware that I had just put away, because
she was unable to find a spoon that she needed and she wondered whether it could be in the box. Just at this moment my
father handed me another pile of books. "Better get a cleaver
and chop me into two," I said.

It was then I realized neither of them was listening to what I
was saying. I had made this remark several times, but I was the

only person who seemed to have heard it. I made up my mind to leave, for I felt I just could not keep muddling through like this. A week had passed since we'd moved from our original home to this new apartment, and every day I was spending all my time getting things organized, and the whole place was full of the smell of paint and the dust was getting up my nose. I am just twenty-four, but here I was, busy the whole week through like someone in middle age. I can't be parted too long from the youthful life, so I took up a position halfway between the kitchen and the study and announced to my parents, "I can't help you any further. I have to go out and attend to some business."

They heard this all right. My father came to the door of the study. "What business?" he asked.

"Something important, of course."

For the moment I was unable to find a compelling justification for leaving, so I could only make this evasive response. My father stepped out of his study and persisted with his question. "What's so important?"

I waved my hand and persisted with my vague excuse. "Whatever it is, it's important."

At this point my mother chipped in. "Are you trying to get out of things?"

"He's trying to get out of it," she told my father. "He's always been like this. After dinner he wants to go to the bathroom, and it'll be two hours before he comes out. Why? To avoid doing the dishes."

"This time it has nothing to do with going to the bathroom," I said.

My father smiled. "Tell me, what is it you have to do? Who are you going to see?"

At that moment I really didn't know how to respond. Fortunately, my mother did something silly. She forgot what she had just been saying. "Who else could it be?" she blurted out. "Apart from those guys Shen Tianxiang, Wang Fei, Chen Liqing, and Lin Meng, who else could he be going to see?"

I took advantage of the possibility presented. "Lin Meng," I said, "is precisely the person I need to go and see."

"What do you need to see him about?" My father was not about to do anything silly. He was going to carry on grilling me.

I began to spin him a line. "Lin Meng got married. His wife's name is Pingping . . ."

"They've been married three years already," my father said.

"That's right," I said. "The thing is, they've been happy together all this time, but now there's trouble . . ."

"What kind of trouble?"

"What kind of trouble?" I thought for a minute. "You know, the kind of trouble that happens in a marriage . . ."

"What kind of trouble in a marriage?" My father still wouldn't let me off the hook.

It was my mother who spoke up then. "They've got to be quarreling over something."

"That's right, they're quarreling," I said.

"If the two of them are quarreling, what's it got to do with you?" My father grabbed me by the sleeve and tried to pull me into the study.

I resisted. "They've started to fight," I said.

My father loosened his grip, and he and my mother looked at me. At this point I was suddenly inspired and began to explain things with effortless fluency:

"It was Lin Meng who first slapped Pingping in the face. Then she fell on him and took a big bite out of his arm. She bit a big hole in his shirt and must have done a lot of damage underneath, because her canine teeth are sharper than bayonets. She must have spent a full three minutes biting him, and Lin Meng was in such pain he was screaming like a stuck pig the whole time. When those three minutes were up, Lin Meng gave Pingping a taste of his fist and his foot. He punched her in the face and kicked her on the leg, and Pingping was in such pain she collapsed on the sofa and couldn't say a word for ten minutes. After that, she really lost her marbles, picking up everything she could lay her hands on and throwing it at Lin Meng. She was so crazy, now it was his turn to be frightened. When she smashed a chair against his midriff, it didn't actually hurt that much, but Lin Meng pretended to keel over in agony, collapsing on the sofa and clutching his belly. He thought Pingping would change her tune when she saw him in this state, that she would stop hitting him, that she would run over and hug him and burst into tears. But what happened was that Pingping, seeing his eyes were closed, picked up an ashtray and smashed it on his head. Now Lin Meng really did faint . . ."

Finally, I said to my stupefied parents, "As a friend of Lin Meng, I should go and see him, don't you think?"

THEN I WAS WALKING along the street, on my way to see these two old friends of mine. I had gotten to know one of them when I was five, the other when I was seven. They were both four years older than me. When they married three years ago, I gave them a blanket as a present, and they sleep under this blanket in the spring—and in the autumn too—so sometimes before they fall asleep they will suddenly think of me and say, "It's almost a month since we last saw so-and-so . . ."

I hadn't seen them for a month, and now as I walked toward

them I began to miss them. First of all, I thought of their little home with its cute decorations, the dozen or so balloons that they tied to the windows, from the ceiling, and beside the chest of drawers. I didn't have a clue why these two loonies were so fond of balloons—and pink ones too. I remembered once, when I was sitting on their sofa, I happened to notice there were three pink panties hanging on the line on the balcony, practically the same color as the balloons, and I figured these had to be Pingping's panties. My first impression had been that they were three balloons, and I was almost about to say that there were balloons hanging on the balcony too. Fortunately I didn't say that, for I'd realized on closer inspection that they weren't balloons at all.

I liked them both. Lin Meng is the kind of person who talks and laughs very loudly. Nine months of the year he wears a brown jacket, and the other three months, because it is so hot, he wears something else. Then his bones stick out and his arms dangle loosely as he walks along the street, so it always seems as though there's empty space inside his clothes.

He is the kind of person who doesn't know his own weaknesses. He has a tendency to stutter, for example, but he himself doesn't realize this, or at least he has never acknowledged it. His wife, Pingping, is a good-looking woman. She has long hair, but most of the time she wears it up. Aware that her neck is slender and pretty, she sometimes wears clothes with high collars, and once her neck is concealed it is even more beautiful, for the high collar looks like a flower petal.

Four years ago, there was nothing going on between them, they were just acquaintances. None of us had any idea how they got together. It was me who made the discovery.

That particular evening I was really bored. First I went to

see Shen Tianxiang, but his mother said he had gone out at lunchtime and was still not back. Then I went to see Wang Fei, and found him lying in bed all flushed, burned to a frizzle by the soaring temperatures. Finally I went to Chen Liqing's home, and he was pounding the table and having a big row with his father. My foot never crossed his threshold, because I didn't want to get involved in other people's quarrels, especially not one between a father and son.

I went back out onto the street again, and just as I was wondering where to go next, I caught sight of Lin Meng. He was walking along under the trees with a quilt under his arm. Although the leaves obscured the light from the streetlamps, I recognized him immediately and called his name. I was so pleased by our fortuitous meeting that my voice seemed unusually loud. "Lin Meng," I said, "I was just about to go and see you."

Lin Meng's head swiveled in my direction, then turned away. I quickened my pace to catch up with him. "Lin Meng, it's me," I called once more.

This time his head kept looking straight ahead, and I had to run forward and clap him on the shoulder. He glanced at me and gave a bad-tempered grunt. It was only then I realized Pingping was walking by his side, a bottle of water in her hands. She gave me a little smile.

Later, they got married. Their married life was happy, so far as I could tell. In the early days we would often run into each other on the steps of the cinema, or sometimes at the entrance to a shop, when I was passing by and they were coming out.

In the first two years of their marriage, I visited their home a few times, and each time I would run into Shen Tianxiang or Wang Fei or Chen Liqing, or all three of them at the same time. We felt very much at home at Lin Meng's place. We could sit on the sofa, or sit on their bed with their quilt folded up behind us for comfort. Wang Fei would often go and open the door of their refrigerator to see what was inside—not, he said, because he was hungry, but simply to have a look.

Lin Meng is a cheerful kind of guy. He uses as his teacup a large glass jar, the kind designed to hold instant coffee, and he likes to plunk a chair down next to the door and sit there with his back against the door, holding that big jar in his hands and laughing his head off as he talks. In no time at all he starts to bullshit. Often he would divulge indiscreet details about his and Pingping's private life, and he got a kick out of this. He'd laugh so much he'd knock his head against the door with a resounding thump.

At such moments Pingping would scowl at him and say, "Don't talk about that."

When there were a lot of people in the room, Pingping would sit on a little round stool, her hands on her knees, watching us talk with a smile on her lips. When we felt maybe we were neglecting her and asked, "Pingping, why don't you say anything?" she would say, "I enjoy listening to you guys talk."

Pingping liked to listen to me summarizing the plot of some recent movies, or Shen Tianxiang telling fishing stories, or Wang Fei comparing different brands of refrigerators, or Chen Liqing singing one of the latest hit songs. What she did not enjoy was Lin Meng's conversation. It wouldn't take long for her husband to say, "Pingping wants to fall asleep in my arms every night."

Pingping's eyebrows would arch in a frown. We would burst

out laughing, and Lin Meng would point at his wife and say, "If I don't take her in my arms, she won't be able to sleep.

"But once I take her in my arms," Lin Meng would continue, "she starts breathing down my neck. It tickles . . ."

At this point, Pingping would say, "Don't talk about that."

"Then it's me who's unable to sleep." Lin Meng would give a big laugh and finish what he wanted to say.

The problem was, Lin Meng's comments on this subject would continue, and would not stop so long as we were there. He's the kind of guy who likes to have us gathered round him, rolling about in stitches, and he would stop at nothing to achieve this kind of effect. He would recite the complete catalog of nicknames that Pingping gave him when they were in bed, leaving us doubled up in laughter.

The list began with "Darling," followed by "Precious," "Prince," "Knight," and "Horsie." Those were the more refined names. Then there were the ones inspired by food items, like "Cabbage," "Tofu," "Sausage," and "Potato," and also some names that we found peculiar, like "Perky" and "Droopy."

"Do you know why she calls me 'Perky'?"

He knew we didn't understand, so he stood up when he asked us this, very full of himself. Pingping got to her feet also. She looked furious and had gone completely pale. "Lin Meng!" she cried.

We were expecting her to really let loose, but all she said was "That's enough."

Lin Meng sat back down with a long belly laugh and looked her in the eye. She returned his gaze, then turned and disappeared into another room. All of us felt very uncomfortable, but Lin Meng acted as though nothing had happened, waving his hand dismissively. "Never mind her," he said.

He then returned to his question. "Do you know what she means by 'Perky'?"

Not waiting for us to shake our heads, he pointed below his belt. "This guy here."

We began to laugh. "And 'Droopy'?" he asked.

This time our eyes automatically fixed on his crotch, and he pointed at the spot again. "Same thing."

It's true what they say, you just have to be prepared to make adjustments when you're married. After Pingping had lived with Lin Meng for a couple of years, she had gotten used to her husband's bullshitting, and when his tongue was wagging she would no longer say to him "That's enough," but would look down and play with her fingers, already resigned, it seemed, to Lin Meng's indiscretions.

Not only that, but on occasion she would make some similar comments herself—of a much more restrained kind, needless to say. I remember one day when we were sitting in their house and everybody was saying how charming Lin Meng looked when he laughed, Pingping broke in: "It's when he's happy at night that he looks his best."

We didn't immediately pick up on what she meant, and we looked at Lin Meng and then at Pingping, unsure whether to laugh. "When he needs me," she added, for clarification.

We had a good laugh at that, and Pingping, realizing she had said something she shouldn't have, flushed bright red. Now that he had become the object of amusement, Lin Meng gave a weak, embarrassed chuckle, and he did not knock his head against the door as usual. He went quiet whenever somebody made a joke at his expense.

So we knew one or two things about their sex life, and even more about other aspects of their marriage. Lin Meng was a lucky man, in our view. Everyone agreed that Pingping was an attractive woman, and it was obvious how understanding and capable she was and we had never seen her get into an argument with Lin Meng over anything. When we visited them, she would always be prompt in pouring water into our teacups and quick to deliver matches to any pair of hands that was preparing to light up a cigarette. After Lin Meng got married, his leather boots were always shining and he dressed with increasingly good taste, all thanks to Pingping. In the past, he had been the most slovenly member of our circle.

SO THERE I WAS, recalling these vignettes of them as a couple, and when I arrived at their apartment on this particular morning, it seemed to me it had been a long time since I had last visited. When Pingping opened the door, I found that she had changed. She had put on some weight, it seemed, or maybe she had lost some.

It was Pingping's hand I saw first. A slender hand grasped the frame, and then the door opened. When Pingping saw me she seemed to give a start—because she hadn't seen me for a long time, I assumed. I walked in with a smile on my face, only to discover there was no sign of Shen Tianxiang or Wang Fei or Chen Liqing—no sign of Lin Meng, even. "Lin Meng?" I inquired.

Lin Meng was not at home. He had left for the factory at seven thirty in the morning. Shen Tianxiang, Wang Fei, and Chen Liqing would also be at work at this hour. There was only me and Pingping . . . "Is it just the two of us?" I said to her.

In the apartment, was what I meant. I noticed how Pingping's face tightened when I said this and I thought to myself, Is that a smile? "What's the matter?" I asked.

Pingping looked at me uncomprehendingly. "Were you smiling at me just now?" I said.

Pingping nodded. "Yes."

Her skin tightened once again. It was me who smiled then. "Why do you smile in such a strange way?" I said.

All this time Pingping had been standing in the doorway. She had never closed the door and her hand was still clutching the doorframe. Her posture seemed to indicate she was simply waiting for me to leave. "Do you want me to go?" I said.

At this, she detached herself from the doorframe and turned to face me, her hands moving this way and that as though she couldn't find a suitable place to put them. I had never seen Pingping in this state, standing completely rigid, her smile unrecognizable as a smile. "What's up with you today?" I said. "Are you about to go out or something?"

She shook her head helplessly. "If you're not in a hurry," I said, "I'll sit down." I sat down in the sofa but she kept on just standing there. I laughed. "What are you doing?" I asked.

She sat down in a chair, her face angled away from me. She was breathing heavily, it seemed, and her legs stirred restlessly, as unable to find a comfortable position as her hands had been just a minute before. "Pingping, what's the matter with you?" I said. "Today I come to visit, and you don't pour me a glass of water and you don't peel me an apple—are you tired of me, or what?"

Pingping shook her head vigorously. "No, not at all. Why would I be tired of you?"

She smiled, and got up and fetched me a glass of water.

This time her smile looked like a smile. "We don't have apples today," she said, passing me the glass. "Would you like a prune?"

"I don't eat prunes," I said. "That's something you women like. Just water is fine."

Pingping sat down in the chair again, and as I sipped my water I said, "In the past, every time I came to your house, I would always find Shen Tianxiang and the others here, or if they weren't all three here, at least one of them was bound to be. Today, not one of them has come, and even Lin Meng is not at home, so it's just the two of us, and you're not a great talker . . ."

Pingping was all keyed up, I suddenly realized. Her head had swiveled round in the direction of the door, and she was listening to something, listening, apparently, to the footsteps of someone coming up the stairs. They walked with a very slow step. They seemed to be in no hurry. They reached the landing just outside, then continued up the next flight of stairs. Pingping exhaled, then turned to look at me. Her face was so pale it gave me a shock. She smiled again, the way that made her skin tighten. I couldn't stand to look at her smile, so instead I glanced around the room. The balloons had disappeared. No pink colors anywhere, so far as I could see, and I couldn't help but take a quick glance at the balcony, but Pingping had no panties hanging there, so there was no pink there either. "Do you not like balloons anymore?" I asked.

Pingping's eyes were watching me in a way that gave me a feeling she heard my voice but didn't hear what I was saying. "The balloons are gone," I said.

"Balloons?" She looked baffled.

"That's right, balloons," I said. "Didn't you used to have lots of balloons hanging in your apartment?"

"Oh . . ." She remembered.

"I get the feeling," I said, "that today you're acting a little . . . How shall I put it? A little strange."

"No, I'm not." She shook her head.

Her denial didn't seem very confident. "I wasn't originally planning to come and see you, did you know that?" I said. "We've moved to a new place, and I was helping my mother to get things sorted out in the kitchen and helping my father to get things sorted out in the study, and they were both driving me crazy the way they were bossing me about, so I hotfooted it out of there, and at first I had the idea of going to see Shen Tianxiang, but he and I were together just a couple of days ago, and I often hang out with Wang Fei and Chen Liqing, so you two were the only people I hadn't seen for a long time. That's why I came to your apartment, not realizing Lin Meng wouldn't be home. I'd forgotten he'd be at work today."

I didn't reveal that I had made up a story about her and Lin Meng having a fight. Pingping was a serious person. "It didn't occur to me you'd be at home on your own . . ."

Finding Pingping alone and so preoccupied, I thought I really should leave. I stood up. "I'll be off now," I said.

Pingping got to her feet at once. "Why don't you stay a bit longer?"

"No, I should go."

She said nothing more and simply stood there waiting. It looked increasingly as though she wanted me out of there right away, and I took a couple of steps toward the door. Then a thought occurred to me. "I'll just use your bathroom."

"There are no public toilets on your street," I added, closing the door behind me.

Originally I was just going to have a pee, but after I'd finished peeing I felt like having a crap, so it was going to take me a while. Just after I squatted down, I heard a thudding outside as though someone was running upstairs at high speed. There was a cry of "Pingping, Pingping!" as he reached the door to the apartment.

It was Lin Meng. I heard Pingping saying, with a quiver in her voice, "How come you're back?"

The door must have opened; Lin Meng had come in. "Today I was sent out to pick up a shipment," I heard him say. "I was desperate for a pee, but I couldn't find a toilet anywhere on the road, so I had to rush back home."

Lin Meng seemed to charge like a wild boar toward the bathroom. As he tugged at the bathroom door, he suddenly went quiet. He must have been shocked to find the door locked, and I heard him ask Pingping in a flustered voice, "Is there someone in there?"

Pingping must have nodded, for the next thing I heard was Lin Meng bellowing, "Who's in there?"

Inside the bathroom, I couldn't help but grin. Before I had the chance to reply, Lin Meng started kicking the door and shouting, "Come out of there!"

At this stage, I had only just squatted down and had had no time to do my business, but given how the door was shuddering under the impact of his kicks I had no choice but to pull up my pants, fasten my belt, and open the bathroom door. When Lin Meng saw it was me, he was dumbfounded. "Lin Meng, I haven't finished yet," I said, "but you were kicking the door so loud. I was about to dump my load, but with you kicking like that, it went back in again."

Lin Meng stared at me, his eyes as big as saucers. "I never expected it would be you!" he said, through clenched teeth.

His expression made me laugh out loud. "Don't look at me that way," I said.

But Lin Meng just carried on staring, and pointed at me, as well. I kept my distance from his extended forefinger. "You're giving me the shivers," I said.

"It's you who's giving *me* the shivers!" Lin Meng roared.

His shouting so alarmed me that I began to take his indignation seriously. "What's the matter?" I asked.

"I had no idea you would carry on with my wife," he said.

"Carry on?" I said. "What do you mean 'carry on'?"

"Cut out the playacting," he said.

I threw a glance at Pingping, hoping to get some idea of what Lin Meng was on about, but I found her face had gone completely white, like a sheet of paper, with just a trace of gray around her lips. The way she looked made me even more uneasy. Now I understood what Lin Meng had in mind. He thought I had slept with Pingping. "Lin Meng," I said, "you're making a big mistake. There's absolutely nothing going on between me and her."

I saw that she was nodding, but Lin Meng seemed not to have the slightest interest in my declaration or in her nod. He pointed at me. "You can give up trying to deny it," he said. "As soon as I came in the door, I could see she was acting strange. Right away I knew there was something fishy going on."

"No," I said. "What you think happened didn't happen at all."

"It didn't happen?" He took a step forward. "Why were you hiding in the bathroom?"

"I wasn't hiding in the bathroom," I said.

He pointed at the bathroom. "What's this—the kitchen?"

"It's not the kitchen, it's the bathroom," I said. "But I wasn't hiding there, I was having a crap."

"Bullshit!" With this, he ran over to the toilet and took a look down, then stood triumphantly by the door. "Why don't I see any crap?" he said.

"I didn't have time to do it," I told him. "The way you were kicking the door, it wouldn't come out."

"Who are you trying to kid?" He waved his hand contemptuously, and then spun on his heel and dived into the bathroom, slamming the door shut, and I heard him saying inside, "The two of you have got me so mad I'm losing my senses. I practically forgot I was dying for a pee."

I could hear his urine splattering on the toilet. I took a look at Pingping. She was now sitting on a chair. Her face was buried in her hands and her shoulders were trembling. I went over to her. "What on earth is happening?" I asked. "I still don't get what's going on."

Pingping raised her head and looked at me. There were tears on her face now, but what really struck me was her look of sheer panic. It seemed as though she wasn't really clear what was happening either. At this moment the bathroom door was thrown open. When Lin Meng came out, it was as if he were a different person, calmed by his peeing. "Sit down," he said to me.

I remained standing. He gave a smile that I didn't expect. "Have a seat," he repeated. "Why not?"

He spoke in a tone that would have made you think nothing at all had happened. My thoughts in an uproar, I sat down next to Pingping. Next thing, Lin Meng came over with pen and paper in his hand and sat down too. "You've let me down," he said to Pingping.

She looked up. "No, I haven't."

Lin Meng ignored her. "You've let me down," he continued, "but I'm not going to beat you, and I'm not going to call you names."

"I haven't," Pingping repeated. "I haven't let you down."

Lin Meng was losing patience. He waved his hand in the air. "No matter what you say, I'm sure you've let me down, so stop all this nonsense! Just keep quiet and listen to what I'm going to tell you. We can't go on living together, do you understand?"

Pingping looked at him, bewilderment on her face. He glanced at me and went on. "Is that clear? You and I have to get divorced, there's no other way out."

Tears streamed down Pingping's face. "Why do we have to get divorced?" she said.

Lin Meng pointed at me. "You've gone to bed with him. Of course I've got to divorce you."

"I didn't," she said.

At this stage, Pingping was still presenting her rebuttals in just the faintest of voices. I wasn't at all happy about that. "You need to say it more forcefully," I told her. "Say it to him loud and clear, there's nothing going on between you and me. Bang the table if you like."

Lin Meng laughed. "It's useless, no matter how loudly she says it. How does it go? With right on your side, you can get anywhere; without it, you'll get nowhere."

"In this case it's we who're in the right," I said, "you who's in the wrong."

Lin Meng gave another laugh. "Did you hear that?" he said to Pingping. "He's saying 'we,' you and him. After I have divorced you, the two of you can get married."

Pingping raised her head and looked at me. Her glance seemed like that of a woman who has just spotted a new partner. I waved my hand. "Pingping, don't listen to his bullshit," I said.

Pingping looked at her husband. He had begun to make marks on the paper with his pen. "I've worked it all out," he said to her. "Our entire savings and cash on hand amount to 12,400 yuan. We each get 6,200. You take your choice of the TV or the VCR, and you can have your pick of the refrigerator and the washing machine . . ."

Seeing as how they were now discussing the division of property, I thought I shouldn't hang around. "I'll leave you to it," I said. "I'm off."

As I headed for the door, Lin Meng seized me by the arm. "You can't leave now," he said. "You've ruined our marriage, and now you have to face up to your responsibilities."

"I didn't ruin your marriage," I said. "I haven't ruined anyone's marriage. What responsibilities do you want me to face up to?"

Lin Meng stood up and pushed me back into the chair where I'd just been sitting. Then he continued to discuss the division of property with Pingping. "Our own clothes, we take with us. The furniture we also divide equally. Of course, we need to apportion them reasonably—we can't split the bed and the table in half . . . This apartment we don't divide—it was yours before we got married, so you get to keep it."

Then he turned to me and issued the following instruction: "After I have divorced Pingping, you have to marry her within a month."

"You've no right to say that to me," I said. "Whether you and Pingping divorce or not has got nothing to do with me."

"You seduced her, you corrupted her, you induced her to commit adultery, and you're telling me it's got nothing to do with you?"

"I didn't seduce her," I said. "Ask Pingping: Did I or did I not seduce her?"

We looked at her. She shook her head back and forth. "Pingping, say it," I said. "Did I or didn't I?"

"You didn't," she said.

But she said this in the feeblest of voices. "Pingping, when you say this kind of thing," I told her, "you need to be assertive. You mustn't be so weak. When Lin Meng humiliates you in front of us, all you do is murmur, 'That's enough.' You should stand up and issue a stinging rebuke."

At this point, Lin Meng patted me on the back. "As a friend," he said, "I want to give you some advice. Don't try to convert Pingping into a shrew, because you're going to be her husband in the future."

"No, I'm not." I said.

"You're going to have to be."

Lin Meng said this with such firm assurance that it quite unnerved me. Once again I turned to Pingping. "Just what is going on here? When I left my house, I had absolutely no idea of bringing a wife back with me—a woman, what's more, who is the wife of a friend of mine. That would be bad enough, but what's worse is that the woman is previously married and four years older than me. My parents would go ballistic . . ."

"That's not true," Lin Meng said. "Your parents are educated people. They wouldn't be concerned about such things."

"You're wrong there—it's educated people who are the most conservative." I pointed at Pingping. "There's no way my parents would accept her."

"They're just going to have to accept Pingping," Lin Meng said.

"Just what is going on here?" Again I turned to her. "My brains are turning to mush. This is driving me crazy."

Pingping was no longer weeping. "You shouldn't have come here today," she told me. "Having come, you should have left right away."

Pointing at Lin Meng, she went on, "Although you guys are his friends, you don't really know him at all."

That was all she said, but it was enough to make things crystal clear. Now I understood why, as soon as I came in the door, Pingping was at such a loss what to do—it was because Lin Meng was not at home. Pingping was a bundle of nerves because I—a man who was not her husband—was alone with her. At the same time, I realized what kind of person Lin Meng was. "I used to think you were a broad-minded and generous person," I told him. "But what you really are is small-minded and jealous."

"You slept with my wife," he said, "and you expect me to be broad-minded and generous?"

"I want you to know," I said, pointing at his nose, "I'm completely sick of you. No matter what kind of garbage you spout, I can't be bothered to argue with you. Pingping is the only person I'm worried about. I feel I've got her into trouble. I shouldn't have come here today . . ."

Having said this, I started to get excited and waved my hand in the air. "No, I did the right thing by coming today! Pingping, it's good that you and he are getting divorced. It's just a disaster to live with this kind of guy. By coming today, I've rescued you. If I were your husband: one, I would respect you and never say things that would make you uncomfortable; two, I would be understanding and do my best to consider your needs; three, I would be genuinely broad-minded and generous, and not just put on a show; four, I would share the responsibility for household chores and not swagger around like a lord as soon as I get home, the way he does; five, I would never tell anybody else the nicknames that you give me; six, when you fall asleep in my arms every night, I wouldn't be bothered by your breath on my neck; seven, I'm a lot stronger than he is, he's all skin and bones . . ."

I kept going until I'd reached fifteen. After that I ran out of things to say and had to stop. When I took a look at Pingping I found her gazing at me with tears in her eyes, clearly moved by my words. Then I looked at Lin Meng. He was sniggering. "That's good," he said. "You put it so eloquently. I can relax now. I know you'll be good to my ex-wife."

"In saying these things, I don't have any special agenda," I replied. "It doesn't mean I would definitely want to marry Pingping. Whether I marry her is not something just for me to decide. Is that what she would want? I don't know. All I meant was, *if* I were her husband."

I looked at her. "Pingping, isn't that so?"

The trouble was, she mistook my meaning. "I'll be your wife," she said, with tears in her eyes. "After hearing what you said just now, I'm happy to be your wife."

I was struck dumb. What an idiot, I thought. I had laid a trap for myself and jumped right into it. When I saw relief blossoming on Pingping's face, I knew my chances of getting out of this were growing more and more remote. Her beauty was now on full display, her lovely eyes glistening as she gazed at me, the tears still flowing. "Pingping, don't cry," I said.

She raised a hand and brushed away her tears. My head was about to explode, I was so carried away. I was out of my mind now. I found myself saying to Lin Meng, in the tone of Pingping's husband, "It's time you left."

He nodded in agreement. "Right, I should be going."

I watched him as he jubilantly made his escape, and a thought occurred to me. I got the feeling that for ages now this guy had probably been looking forward to this very moment—he just hadn't anticipated it would be me who would take over from him. After Lin Meng left, Pingping and I sat there together for a long time, neither of us saying a word, just thinking. Later, she asked me if I was hungry and whether she should go to the kitchen and prepare something. I shook my head. I wanted her to stay sitting. We sat there silently for a while, and then Pingping asked me if I regretted marrying her. I said no. She asked me what I was thinking about. "I feel as though I'm psychic," I told her.

Pingping didn't understand, so I explained. "When I was leaving the house, I made up a story for my parents about how you and Lin Meng had been in a fight, how you had knocked Lin Meng around until he was black-and-blue, how Lin Meng had knocked you around until *you* were black-and-blue . . . and now the two of you really are getting divorced. Wouldn't you say I was psychic?"

Pingping made no response. I knew she still didn't understand, so I explained more fully, giving her all the details of the story I had cooked up for my mom and dad, including the one about how she had smashed an ashtray on the top of Lin Meng's head. When she heard this, Pingping waved her hand in protest, saying she would never do something like that. I said I knew that, I knew she wouldn't, I knew she wasn't a battleaxe. I was telling her these things only so she would realize I was psychic. Now, she understood. She nodded her head and smiled. But as she nodded I was shaking my head. "Actually, I'm not really psychic," I said. "Though I predicted the discord between you and Lin Meng, I didn't foresee I would end up as your husband."

I looked at Pingping pathetically. "I haven't a clue why I have to get married."

FRIENDS

Kunshan left his house with a toothpick in one hand and a shiny kitchen cleaver in the other. He was threatening to slaughter Shi Gang. "Even if I decide to let him off with his life," he said, "I'm still going to keep a piece of him as a souvenir." As for just where this cut of meat would come from, Kunshan believed this would depend on how good a dodger Shi Gang proved to be.

It was lunchtime as Kunshan walked along the boulevard, chewing his toothpick, his eyes bloodshot, strands of tobacco caught in his mustache. As he walked, his lips were slightly curled and his jacket was open, revealing the work belt he wore inside. People could tell at a glance that he was off to have another fight. They tagged along behind, peppering him with questions. "Who is it?" "Kunshan, who are you after?" "Who is it this time?"

Kunshan cut an imposing figure as he marched along, and his retinue grew steadily more numerous. He came to a stop when he reached the bridge, and loudly spat the toothpick into the river below, then set down the cleaver on the concrete parapet and pulled a pack of Front Gate cigarettes from his pocket. He gave the pack a couple of shakes, and the tips of two cigarettes poked out. With his mouth he extracted one, then struck a match and lit up. He wasn't sure yet in which direction he should go. He knew that to go to Shi Gang's house he would need to turn west after crossing the bridge, and to go to the refinery where he worked he would need to go south.

The problem was he didn't know where Shi Gang would be just then.

As Kunshan inhaled, his nostrils flared. Now he began to scan the crowd of people gathered around him. As he looked grimly at their cheerful features, he noticed a thin bespectacled face. "Hey, you're at the refinery, right?" he asked. The thin face moved closer. "You know Shi Gang?"

The man nodded. "We're in the same shop."

Kunshan soon established Shi Gang was still at work. He looked at his watch. It had just turned one, which meant Shi Gang's shift had now ended and he'd be on his way to the bathhouse. Kunshan smiled thinly and went on leaning against the parapet. He took a few more puffs. It was at this point that he made his comments to the onlookers about slaughtering Shi Gang or, at the very least, chopping off a piece of him.

I was a boy of eleven then, on my way to the refinery. After lunch I had dumped my textbooks onto my bed, stuffed some clean clothes into my satchel along with a towel and soap, and asked my mother for ten fen. "I'm going to take a bath," I told her.

With the satchel on my back I headed off, but not toward the public bathhouse in town. One had to pay for admission there, and I wanted to keep those ten fen for myself, so I headed for the refinery bathhouse instead. It was April, and the parasol trees were laden with broad leaves. The sun shone brightly, catching the dust thrown up from the street.

I left the house at eleven forty-five, having calculated the time carefully. I knew I should arrive at the main entrance to the refinery at twelve noon precisely, for that was when the old gatekeeper would be sitting in the reception office eating his lunch. He wore a pair of glasses with heavy prescription lenses, and I was confident that the steam rising from his bowl would completely obscure his vision. Besides, he liked to bury his head in his food. I regularly slipped in at this time, bending double as I crept underneath his window. At twelve thirty, I would be steeping naked in the refinery's cozy little bathhouse. I would have the place to myself then, and the water would be so hot it would practically scald my bottom and the steam would be so thick it would hang motionless, as though painted on the wall. I would need to be out of there by one o'clock, rinsing off the soap before those greasy workers stepped into the water: when they marched in with their towels over their shoulders, I would have already dried myself, knowing it wouldn't take long for them to fill the water with frothy white bubbles and turn it into bean milk.

But, this particular lunchtime, I stopped when I got to the bridge and lost all sense of time, forgetting that the old gate-keeper at the refinery would soon finish his lunch and then start pacing back and forth in front of the gate with his hands behind his back. It would be ages before he would stump back to his room and sit down, by which point the water in the bath-house would be getting cold.

I stood on the bridge, squeezed between the midriffs of the adults there, watching Kunshan as he leaned against the para-pet, smoking and spitting out large gobs of phlegm. He fasci-nated me, the way his mustache grew above his thick mouth, the way the muscles on his face shook like a flag in the wind when he talked. I was amazed by all the muscle this man had just on his cheeks, and after I'd inspected his chest—a thick chest that even a bayonet would not be able to pierce—and studied his arms and legs, I told myself this Shi Gang character was a goner.

I didn't know Kunshan's last name—nor did many of the locals—but we all knew perfectly well who he was. He was the man who would borrow money from people and not bother to pay them back. When he ran out of smokes, he would stop passersby in the street and cheerfully pat their pockets with his broad palms, and once he had located a pack of cigarettes he would slip a hand into the pocket and extract the cigarettes, offering one to their owner and depositing the remainder in his own pocket. There was nobody in our town who didn't know about Kunshan, and even babies could sense the tingle of fear that his name evoked. But we admired him too, and when we ran into him in the street we would call out his name at the top of our lungs. I was already doing that by the time I was five, and the habit had stuck with me ever since. Was this why, when Kunshan was walking along the street, he was always beaming with satisfaction? He liked it when people greeted him and would always give a gracious response. He found it pleasing that everyone in town showed him proper respect.

Kunshan now tossed the cigarette butt into the river and gave a regretful shake of his head. "Shi Gang doesn't show me proper respect."

"Why do you say that?"

Kunshan fixed his gaze on the thin-faced man with the glasses. Slowly his hand rose to the level of the man's head and he made the motion of a box on the ear. "He slapped my wife."

I heard a collective intake of breath and I myself was thrown for a loop, wondering how on earth someone could dare do that. Then somebody asked the question uppermost in my mind. "He had the gall to slap your wife? Who does this Shi Gang think he is?"

"I don't know him." Kunshan's finger stabbed the air. "But now I'm eager to meet him."

"Maybe he didn't realize it was your wife he was beating," the thin-faced man said.

Kunshan shook his head. "That's impossible."

Someone else spoke up. "Whether he knew or not, if he beat her, then Kunshan's going to make him pay for it. How could you even dream of beating Kunshan's wife?"

"You're wrong there," Kunshan said. "My wife deserves a beating."

He looked at his dumbfounded audience. "Other people may not know my wife, but I sure do. She really deserves a good beating. With her wicked tongue, she's always going around making a nuisance of herself. If she wasn't married to me, I don't know how many times she would have had her ears boxed . . ."

Kunshan paused for a moment. "But in spite of all that, she's still my wife. If she's done something wrong or spoken out of turn, you can come and see me about it, and if she needs a box on the ears then I'll do it myself. That Shi Gang never breathed a word about it to me, but just went ahead and gave my wife a box on the ears."

Kunshan picked up the cleaver from the parapet and smiled thinly. "If he doesn't show me proper respect, he can't be too surprised if I don't take it kindly."

Kunshan took a step in our direction. We cleared a path for him, and when his massive figure began to move down the street it was as though there was a powerful ship steaming up the river, and we people clustered around him were like the waves thrown up by its screw. Together we marched forward, myself in an excellent position on Kunshan's right. His glinting cleaver swayed back and forth by my shoulder like a swing. This was proving to be an exhilarating lunch break, the first time I had walked among so many grown-ups. By escorting Kunshan, they had become my escorts too. We made a good deal of noise as we advanced and pedestrians came to a halt, watching us curiously and quizzing us. Each time I made sure I was first to answer their inquiries, telling them Kunshan was going to make Shi Gang pay in blood. I drew out the word "blood" especially loud and long, not minding if I made myself hoarse in the process. This attracted Kunshan's attention, and he would occasionally glance down at me, his eyes glowing with amusement. It was my heartfelt hope at this moment that the street leading to the refinery could be as long as night, because as we went I kept running into classmates and their eyes were round with envy. I realized I was making a name for myself. The sunlight shone down directly in our faces, making my eyes narrow to a crack, and when I looked up at Kunshan, his eyes had narrowed too.

We were now approaching the main entrance to the refinery and from a distance I could see the old man from the reception office standing outside. This time he wasn't pacing back and forth with his hands behind his back, but craning his head in our direction like a bird. We walked right up to him and, now that it was obvious he saw me, I suddenly felt frightened, thinking he would very likely come over and grab me by the scruff of the neck, just as my father, my teacher, and my older brother often did. A shiver ran down my spine. I looked up at Kunshan, his face flushed red by the sun, and timidly I cried to the old man, "It's Kunshan!"

To my ears, my voice sounded faint and thin, seeming to quiver like a leaf. But the old man had already retreated to one side, where he watched us with the same curiosity as the other bystanders. Just like that we swaggered in, the old man not making the slightest effort to stand in our way. What a piece of cake, I thought to myself.

We marched along the concrete road, flanked by open workshop doors wider even than the main gate we had just come through. Oil-stained men stood watching us and somebody asked, "Is Shi Gang in the bathhouse?"

"Yes," I heard.

"He's in the bathhouse," somebody said.

"Right, then," said Kunshan.

Past the workshops we turned a corner and there ahead of us was the cafeteria, and off to one side was the tall chimney of the boiler room, spewing thick smoke that swirled up in billowing clouds before dispersing in the clear sky. Two boiler workers stood watching us, leaning on their iron shovels as though they were walking sticks. We strode past them and on to the bathhouse. Some people had just emerged from the building in plastic flip-flops and clutching their work clothes, their hair still dripping, their faces and feet as pink as if they had been cooked. Kunshan came to a halt. We all came to a halt. Kunshan said to the thin face with the glasses, "Go and check whether Shi Gang is inside."

The man went inside, while we waited. More people crowded around us and the two boiler workers came over, dragging their shovels behind them. "Kunshan, who are you looking for?" one of them asked. "Who offended you?"

Kunshan said nothing, so someone answered for him. "Shi Gang."

"What did Shi Gang do?"

This time Kunshan himself replied. "He didn't show me proper respect."

His hand slipped into his pocket, felt about a bit, and brought out a cigarette and a box of matches. He stuck the cigarette in his mouth, sandwiched the cleaver under his armpit, and lit the cigarette. The thin-faced man emerged. "Shi Gang is inside," he said. "He's soaping himself."

"Tell him Kunshan has come for him," Kunshan instructed.

"I told him that already," the thin-faced man said. "He said he would be out shortly."

"Shi Gang must be scared shitless," someone said.

The thin-faced man shook his head. "No, he's just soaping himself."

A look of regret appeared on Kunshan's face. I'd seen that look before, on the bridge, when he said he hadn't been shown proper respect. This time he was disappointed because Shi Gang was not as panic-stricken as he had anticipated. "Kunshan, go in and carve him up," someone said. "With his clothes off, he'll be like a plucked chicken."

Kunshan shook his head. "Tell him I'll give him five minutes. Any more than that and I'll go in and fetch him out."

The thin-faced man went inside again. There was a buzz of conversation around me, but Kunshan stood silent. His cigarette was clamped tightly between his lips, and its smoke made his right eye squint.

The thin-faced man came out. "Shi Gang says not to worry. He says five minutes is plenty."

People were smiling, looking forward to the moment when Shi Gang would come out and trade blows with his adversary. Kunshan's face darkened and his cheek muscles tightened. He nodded. "Okay, I'll wait."

It was then I left him, abandoning the vantage point I had been steadfastly defending for so long. Many times someone or other had tried to elbow me away from my place next to Kunshan, and only with the utmost effort had I been able to retain my position. But Shi Gang so intrigued me I just had to take a look in the bathhouse. There, amid the hot steam, I saw a dozen or so people soaking in the bath and a few others standing around the edge with their clothes on. I could hear them talking about the impending showdown. I studied them carefully, unsure which was Shi Gang. I remembered the thin-faced man had said he was soaping himself, so I had a look at the wiry, broad-shouldered man who was standing in the middle of the bath, wiping soap from his hair with a towel. After brushing away the soap, he sat down on the edge of the bath and rubbed his face. The soap had run into his eyes and he rubbed them a bit, then twisted his towel dry and gave them another gentle rub. I heard someone call Shi Gang's name. "Do you want us to help you?" he asked.

"No need."

It was the man rubbing his eyes who answered, so I knew I'd identified him correctly. I watched with excitement as he got up and walked toward me, still toweling his hair. I made no effort to step aside, and when he bumped into me he put out a supporting hand, as though concerned I might fall over.

Then he went into the changing room. I followed him, and so did the people who were already dressed. I watched as Shi Gang dried himself and unhurriedly put on a shirt and trousers. Then he sat down on a bench, slipped his feet into his shoes, and began to tie his shoelaces. "Do you really not want us to help?" somebody asked.

"No need." He shook his head.

He got to his feet, and took down a canvas boiler suit that was hanging on the wall. He rolled it up and wrapped it around his left arm as though it was a bandage, and with his left hand he took a tight grip of the two loose ends. Then, picking up his towel, he went over to a tap, turned on the water, and thoroughly soaked the towel.

It was afternoon by this time, and the shadows had begun to lengthen, so now the spot where Kunshan and the others stood was in the shade. They watched as Shi Gang emerged into the bright sunlight. With the rolled-up boiler suit wrapped around his elbow it looked almost as though he had a basketball tucked under his arm. His right hand gripped the sodden towel, which dripped water like a leaky tap and made a damp patch on the ground.

I had been standing next to Shi Gang, and when I noticed that the people next to Kunshan were beginning to withdraw, I retreated a couple of steps and took shelter underneath a tree. Kunshan marched two steps forward, leaving the shadows for the sunlight. He squinted at Shi Gang, and I looked at him too. The sunshine illuminated him from behind, making his hair gleam. But no light fell on his face and he did not squint, but looked at Kunshan with a frown.

Kunshan took the cigarette from his mouth and tossed it

on the ground. "So you're Shi Gang," he said. The other man nodded. "Is Shi Lan your sister?"

Shi Gang nodded again. "That's right."

Kunshan smiled. He transferred the cleaver from his right hand to his left and took another step forward. "You're a big boy now," he said. "Quite a nerve you've got, too." As he said this, he swung a fist at Shi Gang, who ducked the blow. Kunshan looked at him in surprise. "Playing hard to get, are we?" he said.

He aimed a kick at Shi Gang's knee with his right foot, but Shi Gang jumped out of the way, once again neutralizing the threat. A look of astonishment appeared on Kunshan's face. He chuckled, then glanced at us spectators. "He's good."

As he turned his head, Shi Gang went into action. He lashed Kunshan's face with the dripping towel and we heard a huge, resounding slap, louder by far than the sound of a hand hitting a face. Kunshan gave a yelp, and the cleaver fell to the ground. He clutched his face with his right hand and stood rooted to the spot. Shi Gang took two steps back and twisted the towel tightly once more, then fixed his eyes on his opponent. When Kunshan spread his arms, we saw that beads of water now spotted his face; his left eye and cheek were bright red. He bent down to pick up the cleaver, grasping it in his right hand while clutching his face with his left. Brandishing the cleaver he flailed out at Shi Gang and, when Shi Gang took evading action once again, Kunshan kicked him in the leg, forcing him to beat such a hasty retreat that he almost slipped and fell. No sooner had he regained his footing than the cleaver was again arcing toward him. With no time to get out of the way, Shi Gang raised the arm encased in the boiler suit. Kunshan's cleaver thudded into his arm, and at the same moment Shi Gang's towel smacked Kunshan in the face.

I have never seen such a ferocious fight. Time and again the cleaver thudded into Shi Gang's arm, and time and again the towel whacked Kunshan's face. The canvas boiler suit served as Shi Gang's shield; when he couldn't dodge he could at least raise his arm. Kunshan used his left hand to ward off Shi Gang's weapon: when the soaking towel whipped toward his face, it just as often hit his hand. The two men leapt back and forth between the sunlight and the shade, like fighting crickets in the thick of mortal combat. Again and again we heard howls of pain, and their hoarse pants grew heavier and heavier, but they showed no signs of stopping and seemed to want to fight to the bitter end.

During the course of the battle, my bladder got so bloated I had to pee. I couldn't find a toilet in the refinery, so I dashed out into the boulevard and had to run practically all the way to the ferry wharf before I found one. On my return I forgot about the old man's sentry duty at the entrance, and when I raced in through the gate I thought I heard him shouting and cursing behind me, but I couldn't care less. When I finally made it back to the bathhouse they were still engaged in their unremitting struggle, thank God.

I have never seen such a protracted fight or such tireless protagonists. The way they jumped back and forth, they must practically have run the marathon. Some felt they couldn't afford to wait for the final outcome and left, only to be replaced by others on their way to the night shift, who eagerly seized plum spots where they had a good view of the action. Twice I noticed Shi Gang's towel was so dry it had become a soft and feeble weapon. Each time friends promptly handed him a newly soaked replacement. Shi Gang would then lash Kunshan's puffy face so that it swelled all the more, while Kunshan's cleaver sliced the boiler suit on Shi Gang's arm into ribbons of cloth, like the end of a mop. It was then we heard the sounds of stir-frying from the cafeteria next door and I noticed people were clutching mess tins.

Shi Gang's wet towel struck Kunshan's right hand, knocking the cleaver to the ground. This time he stood motionless, looking at Shi Gang as though in a daze. His eyes and face were red and swollen, and it seemed he couldn't see Shi Gang clearly, because when Shi Gang took two steps to his right Kunshan continued to look at the spot where he had been standing. After a moment or two, he took a corner of his jacket and cautiously rubbed his sore eyes. Shi Gang stood to one side, his arms hanging loose, his mouth half open, panting as he watched. A minute later, the towel dropped from his hand, and after eyeing Kunshan a moment longer, Shi Gang raised his right hand and gingerly removed the boiler suit from his left arm. That thick canvas suit was now a bundle of rags. Shi Gang took it off and threw it on the ground. We could then see that his left arm was badly cut up. Clutching his left arm with his right hand, he turned and walked off, several of his friends falling in behind. Kunshan was no longer rubbing his eyes—he was simply blinking, as though to test his vision. It was then I saw the sky had reddened with the glow of sunset.

I had personally witnessed the towel's vanquishing of the blade, and now I knew that a sodden towel could be a formidable weapon. In the days that followed I would always leave the bathhouse with a soaking-wet towel in my hand, and on the long walk home I thought of myself as bold and powerful. I even took my wet towel to school and strutted back and forth on the playground, looking out for troublemakers, and my classmates would cluster around me just as we had clustered around Kunshan. These blissful days carried on for quite some time, until I lost my towel. I never figured out how this happened. It was still dripping wet, and I think I'd hung it over the branch of a tree. All I remember is that we were running around after a ball and later we went home—I never saw the towel again. My mother, always strapped for cash, gave me a tongue-lashing, and my equally hard-up father gave me a couple of slaps on the face, leaving me with aching teeth for a whole week afterward.

Later on, I left the house dejectedly and went for a walk by the riverside, one hand scraping along the parapet. Pink clouds floated in the water, but I was glum and spent, like ashes after a fire. Just as I got to the bridge, I caught sight of Kunshan. The contusions had now gone from his face and he had regained his former air of vitality. He came swaggering along as though he owned the whole town. Suddenly I was filled with excitement, because at the very same moment I saw Shi Gang. He was approaching from the other direction. The arm that had been injured was now swinging casually by his side, and he was heading toward Kunshan.

I felt as though the breath had been knocked out of me, and my heart thumped. Their stirring combat was surely about to resume. But this time there was no cleaver and no towel: their only weapons were their fists and their feet—one was wearing leather shoes, I noticed, the other sneakers. Kunshan went right up to Shi Gang, blocking his way, and I heard him say loudly, "Hey, got a cig?"

Shi Gang didn't answer; he just stood there, eyeing his

adversary. Kunshan began to pat Shi Gang's jacket, then his hand slipped inside a pocket and pulled out a pack of cigarettes. I knew he was being provocative, but still Shi Gang made no move. Kunshan extracted a cigarette, and I thought he would pass it to Shi Gang and keep the rest for himself. But instead he stuck the cigarette in his mouth, looked at Shi Gang, and handed the pack back. Shi Gang took it, extracted a cigarette, and put it between his lips. What happened next took me completely by surprise. Shi Gang slipped the pack into the other man's pocket. Kunshan smiled. He took out his matches, lit Shi Gang's cigarette, then his own.

That evening the two of them leaned against the bridge and there was no end to their banter, no end to their laughter. I watched as the sunset bathed them in a rosy hue, staying on until they were shrouded in darkness. They rested their arms on the parapet, their cigarettes glowing as they held them up to their faces. Though I stood listening just a few feet away, nothing they said really sank in. For a long time afterward, I kept trying to recall the brand of cigarettes they smoked first, but somehow four names would come to mind all at the same time—Front Gate, Flying Horse, People's Choice, and West Lake.

ABOUT THE AUTHOR

Yu Hua is the author of five novels, six collections of stories, and four collections of essays. His work has been translated into more than twenty languages. In 2002, he became the first Chinese writer to win the James Joyce Award. His novel *Brothers* was short-listed for the Man Asian Literary Prize and awarded France's Prix Courrier International. *To Live* was awarded Italy's Premio Grinzane Cavour, and *To Live* and *Chronicle of a Blood Merchant* were ranked among the ten most influential books in China in the 1990s by *Wen Hui Bao,* the largest newspaper in Shanghai. Yu Hua lives in Beijing.

ABOUT THE TRANSLATOR

Allan H. Barr is the translator of Yu Hua's debut novel, *Cries in the Drizzle,* and his essay collection *China in Ten Words.* He teaches Chinese at Pomona College in California.

A NOTE ON THE TYPE

This book was set in Caledonia, a Linotype face designed by W. A. Dwiggins (1880–1956). It belongs to the family of printing types called "modern face" by printers—a term used to mark the change in style of the type letters that occurred around 1800. Caledonia borders on the general design of Scotch Roman but it is more freely drawn than that letter.

COMPOSED BY
NORTH MARKET STREET GRAPHICS, LANCASTER, PENNSYLVANIA
PRINTED AND BOUND BY
BERRYVILLE GRAPHICS, BERRYVILLE, VIRGINIA
DESIGNED BY
IRIS WEINSTEIN